Migration
Patterns

Migration
Patterns

Stories

Gary Schanbacher

Fulcrum Publishing
Golden, Colorado

Grateful acknowledgment is made to the following publications
in which some of these stories were first published: *Colorado Review*,
"Regaining Flight"; *South Dakota Review*, "Windship Universe
Floats to Earth"; *The William and Mary Review*, "Laws of
Gravity"; *Concho River Review*, "Fairweather, Colorado."

Library of Congress Cataloging-in-Publication Data

Schanbacher, Gary L.
    Migration patterns : stories / Gary L. Schanbacher.
        p. cm.
    ISBN 978-1-55591-646-6 (pbk. : alk. paper) 1. West
(U.S.)--Social life and customs--Fiction. I. Title.
    PS3619.C3257M54 2007
    813'.6--dc22
                                    2007021437
Printed in the United States of America by Thomson-Shore, Inc.
0 9 8 7 6 5 4 3 2 1

Editorial: Katie Raymond, Faith Marcovecchio
Cover and interior design: Ann W. Douden
Cover image © Jupiter Images

FULCRUM PUBLISHING
4690 Table Mountain Drive, Suite 100
Golden, Colorado 80403
800-992-2908 • 303-277-1623
www.fulcrumbooks.com

Migration Patterns

With love to my wife, Sherri,
and son, Will,
who never lacked faith and offered
unwavering support

Contents

▶

Storms

Deep into summer, drought withered the land west of the Mississippi while storms lashed the East. Unrelenting rains loosened the earth's hold on century-old maples, and the winds toppled them like bowling pins. Tornadoes sliced through farms and small towns with capricious violence. Long after the flood season, rivers boiled over their banks.

Caitlin was perched at the foot of her bed in a motel room in some small township off of I-64 an hour or so west of New Albany, Indiana, mesmerized by the weather channel on television. Bent at the waist, elbows resting on her knees, she studied the positioning of the isobars on the map with the strategic intensity of a field officer considering the placement of his troops along the battle line.

The commanding general of low-pressure fronts, it occurred to Nash, who watched her from the small table by the door where he practiced arithmetic problems with

▶

her daughter, Darcy. One apple plus two apples, that kind of thing.

Caitlin was still dressed for sleep. In her oversize pullover, baby blue with teddy bears dancing on white clouds, her hair still mussed, and without makeup, she could pass for Darcy's older sister instead of her mother. Indeed, sometimes when they were out together, at the mall, maybe, Caitlin would tell Darcy, "Baby, call me Caitlin. Pretend like we're sisters." And Darcy would say, "Okay, Momma." But she never did; she never called her anything but "momma."

"Look here!" Caitlin called to them, leaping from the bed, running to the television, and sweeping her hand over Texas and Louisiana. She mimicked the weather announcer: "Low pressure from the north colliding with warm, moist air from the gulf."

She walked to Nash, straddled his lap, and sat facing him. "Something big brewing down south," she said, and her thighs tightened around him.

She glanced over her shoulder at Darcy. "Baby, go get two dollars from my purse and get yourself a soda and a candy bar from the machine. Then see if Mari is up yet. You know how she likes to sleep in."

Darcy squealed at her sudden good fortune, jumped from her chair, grabbed the money, and ran for the door.

"Hold on," Nash protested, "that is one horrible idea

for breakfast. Why not—"

But when Caitlin swiveled back to face him and pressed her hips down into his lap, Nash completely lost his train of thought. Before the door shut behind Darcy, Caitlin was working at the belt of his jeans and he was sliding her nightshirt up over those slim hips.

Sex with Caitlin still surprised him. He could not help but wonder why someone so young and sexually charged would be attracted to him, weary around the eyes, twice her age, and every year etched into his face like a road map to a hard life. But he had also lived long enough to accept the good fortune that occasionally came his way without questioning too deeply the why of it, knowing that, sooner rather than later, the good would be repaid three times over with bad.

Afterward, Caitlin sat naked on the bed, hugging her knees to her chest, her attention once again drawn to the television weather report.

Nash had dressed, in the event Darcy returned, and he rested against the headboard and ran his thumb down the ridges of Caitlin's backbone. A small mountain range rose from the smooth plateau of her back, reminding him of the land he had fled, where his life had become as withered as the drought-ridden earth, dry as bone. He was carried for an instant to Colorado and to what he had left behind until the sound of a key working the door lock startled him back to the present.

He rose from the bed and walked across the room as Caitlin reached for her nightshirt. When he opened the door, he found Shea, one of their crew, checking his key against the room number on the wall next to the door-jamb.

"Sorry," Shea said. "Wrong room, I guess."

He appeared disheveled and smelled sour. He stared past Nash, and something like a smile curled his lip. Nash felt the back of his neck redden as he imagined Caitlin smoothing the shift down over her breasts.

"You just getting in?" Nash asked. "You fit to work?"

Shea leveled his eyes on Nash. "I'll be fine. Don't sweat it, Pops."

There was hardness to his stare, like he was challenging Nash to go on with it, and Nash considered it but reined himself and closed the door on the hired hand.

"He needs to go," Nash said to Caitlin. "He's trouble waiting to happen."

"We're shorthanded. He'll do," Caitlin answered, settling back on the bed and refocusing on the television.

"You just wait and see," she said, as if Nash had been disputing her forecast. "There'll be one hell of a storm down there. Louisiana is my guess. We'll have more work than we can handle. Best finish up here and head south."

The general mustering her troops, Nash thought.

They had been in Indiana for the past few weeks, traveling from town to town, making money from the tornadoes that had knifed across the state the previous month.

It is what they did—followed the storms and cleaned up after them, Caitlin and her crew: Nash, Roland, Mari, Shea, and Lyle. Traveling in two Econolines packed with gear and an old Ford 150 pickup, they slept in the vans until they could afford a few rooms at one of the weekly-rate motels when they found a town to work.

They started with the trees. It was an easy sell when they pointed out the cracked limb poised over the power lines, the threat of the next strong gust cutting off their electricity. Working the trees, they noticed damage on the roof; it is amazing how few people ever ventured up the ladder to verify. Then maybe loose chinking around the chimney. Or whatever. It was this part of the job that ate at Nash the most. The crew performed decently clearing away deadfall and pruning trees with the equipment they had, but, except for Nash, they lacked both the knowledge and the ambition for most of the other repairs. Caitlin shrugged off his concern about not providing people with the full services paid for.

"Number one," she would tick down the list while counting on her fingers, "the people can't do it themselves or they wouldn't hire us. Number two, the big companies won't bother with the folk out here in the sticks, so it's us or nothing. And number three," she would say, then thrust her outstretched fingers in his face for emphasis, "the customers know exactly what they are buying. Half of them have me pad the bill so a little of the insurance money flows their way. It's an even trade."

They worked an area fast, in and out, then moved on to the next county, the next storm. Just followed the weather. The thought had crossed Nash's mind that they profited from the misfortune of others, but the easy money, the lack of anywhere better to be, and Caitlin's warm bed kept him on the road.

Nash was convinced they had worn thin their welcome in Indiana. A sheriff's deputy had driven out to the motel last evening and asked them what they knew about the loads of tree trimmings dumped along the side of Route 145. And about a roof patch on a house over in Brown County that was already failing so miserably that plaster had begun raining down into the dining room. So when Caitlin mentioned heading south, Nash suggested they load up right away. But Caitlin had other ideas.

"Still have to finish up the Bellingham place. There's the attic insulation to lay and that sealing work in the basement."

Caitlin had come across Mrs. Bellingham the past week while she was out scouting customers. She had returned to the motel with a case of beer in the bed of the pickup for the crew and in high spirits, like she had already popped a few.

"That lady's house is in need of repair, and she's willing to pay. Didn't bargain with me at all, so I know she's set up. Paid cash for the deposit," she had said, pulling a wad of bills from the pocket of her jeans.

The crew had already trimmed the pin oaks lining her driveway and replaced some rotten window frames, but Nash knew Caitlin was not one to leave money on the table. With her mind set on finishing, the only question was how soon they could wrap things up.

▶ ▶ ▶

Nash knocked on the wall to let Roland and Mari know they were ready to begin the day. By the time he had cranked up one of the vans, they emerged from their room, with Darcy tagging along behind.

Roland and Mari were married and looked like a matched pair, both short and stumpy and slack around the jowls, like two hounds. They could have passed for brother and sister—and, indeed, there was talk of some distant relationship down the line. Watching them lumber toward the van, Nash speculated what they might have looked like when they were teenagers—not that many years ago by the calendar—and what about each had attracted the other. And he thought maybe the truth was that they had ignored one another in high school, each holding out for something better, until life had shucked away their dreams and whatever weak aspirations they might have held, and there they were, the only two kernels left on the cob. You saw people like Roland and Mari every day in discount-store luncheonettes, eating chili-cheese dogs, staring mutely out into space. *And maybe, in a way, they were the lucky ones*, Nash concluded. They had something, at least, and, to his observation, no false expectations about pots of gold at the end of the rainbow.

Roland hopped in beside Nash and nodded a greeting.

Nash called Darcy over to the van and reached into the glove compartment for an orange left over from yesterday's lunch. "Promise me you'll eat some of this before you have any more soda, okay honey?"

"Sure, Nash. When you get home, will you color with me?"

"You bet."

Nash made a mental note to stop for a fresh box of crayons on the way back to the motel that evening. *Home*, she called it. Funny.

Mari slid into the backseat, and they sat waiting for Shea and Lyle. Nash tapped the horn. They waited.

Caitlin came out to the van and ducked her head inside through the front window. "Thanks for watching

Darcy. Nash and I needed to talk private for a bit."

"No problem," Mari said. "Private talk is good for a couple." She poked Roland in the back of his neck, and he looked away across the parking lot. "And you two surely do have your share of conversations lately." She shot Caitlin one of those sideways glances, and Caitlin flashed a grin, pivoted on her heels, and, hand in hand, she and Darcy skipped back to the room.

At the door, Caitlin called over her shoulder, "We'll see you out at the site later!"

Recently, she had begun insisting that Darcy ride along with her while she visited job prospects. "Good for business," she explained, though whenever the two went off together, Nash felt a prick of apprehension, like that of leaving your child with an unfamiliar babysitter. Until recently, it had been Mari's job to look after Darcy when Caitlin went pitching her work.

Finally, Lyle and Shea, whose hair still dripped from the shower, stumbled from their room and climbed into the pickup next to Nash's van.

The two had been a part of Caitlin's crew for only a month, and Nash had little use for them. They replaced two illegals who had hitched a ride into Chicago to visit some relatives and not returned. They had been hard workers, quiet and uncomplaining, but these two new ones Nash judged shiftless, men requiring close supervi-

▶ *Storms*

9

sion so they not cross the line and have the law after them for serious. They both had eyes for Caitlin, so it was easy for her to keep them in tow. Lyle was of no concern to Nash. He had the face of a horse and plodded around like a farm animal. But Shea was another matter. He had the looks to compete: he wore his hair in that long, shaggy style that made Nash conscious of his own thinning crop and was big-boned with a flat stomach and thick across the shoulders and chest. His face was just starting to show the puffy toll of excess drink and drugs, and Nash recognized that before long, women would know to fear him. But for now, he retained just enough of his youth to appear provocative rather than dangerous, and his eyes held that cocky self-confidence that Nash knew appealed to some women. More than once, Nash had caught Shea in an aggressive, openly sexual appraisal of Caitlin, and more than once, he had noticed her responding with a flirtatious glance or a feline stretch.

Once Shea and Lyle settled into the pickup, Nash led the crew out onto the highway toward Mrs. Bellingham's place.

She lived alone in an old farmhouse—two stories, stone foundation, weathered wood siding, windows everywhere, and a gabled roof. Shrouded by oaks, the house sat at the end of a long gravel driveway and was surrounded by corn and soybean fields she leased to neighboring farmers.

Mrs. Bellingham had that healthy Midwestern plumpness to her, like she had lived her life in the kitchen cooking for field hands. But to Nash, she seemed to have an edge to her as well, a no-nonsense self-sufficiency that he imagined came from long years spent living on her own. After Shea and Lyle took a two-hour lunch break the first day on the job and returned smelling of beer, Mrs. Bellingham decided to provide sandwiches for the crew right there at the house and threatened to send them "down the road" if it happened again. Caitlin made a point thereafter to spend time visiting with her on the porch each day, and she made a point of having Darcy with her.

"We'll be just fine," Caitlin explained to Nash, "as long as me and Darcy keep Mrs. Bellingham company and you keep the crew in line."

But because Mrs. Bellingham watched their work closely, the repairs were taking longer than suited Caitlin.

Out at the house, the morning passed as usual. On the roof, Shea worked his way up and over the peak to the opposite side of Nash, where he stripped off his T-shirt, rolled it into a pillow, and dozed in the sun. Here and there, Nash replaced damaged shingles with mismatched and low-grade discards that Mari and Roland had scrounged from the dump pile of a building site they had located somewhere around Evansville. They had a knack for sniffing out unfenced construction sites, recent demolitions, and landfills that contained scrap material. They would take the pickup out at night and return later with a load of whatever the crew required for the next day's job.

Roland and Mari unloaded the pickup. While Roland ferried the shingles from the truck up to the roof, Lyle stood by the pickup, carefully inspecting every inch of its rust-pocked frame with a concentration that reminded Nash of Darcy searching inside that big picture book for where in the world Waldo might be. Lyle performed this ritual almost every day, and eventually he would find something that needed immediate attention. He would call up to them, "Got a slow leak, right front tire! I'll just run it over to a station and have it patched," and that would be the last the crew saw of him until lunchtime.

They were not on the roof for more than a few hours when Mrs. Bellingham called them down for dinner.

Dinner, country talk that touched Nash in some way, comforted him with vague memories of his own grandparents, who had raised winter wheat and a few cattle northeast of Denver until the down market in the sixties forced them out.

Mrs. Bellingham provided stacks of sandwiches holding leftover meats and fresh vegetables from her garden. Following their initial run-in, Shea and Lyle had been working her like she was the farmer's daughter and they two hicks fresh off the hay wagon.

"I do believe this is the tastiest catfish (or meatloaf, or turkey, or whatever happened to be stuffed between two slabs of homemade bread) I have ever eaten," Shea would say, flashing Mrs. Bellingham his best smile while Lyle nodded and made a show of licking his fingers.

Mrs. Bellingham did not buy a word of it, Nash could tell, but several days of compliments did seem to ease her suspicion of the two. For the most part, Nash and Roland, and Mari, when she was around, ate under the shade of the big persimmon tree in the front yard and carried their plates to the kitchen when they were done. That day, when Nash took the dishes inside, Shea was standing at the sink, drying glasses that Mrs. Bellingham had washed. They looked like best pals.

After lunch, back on the roof, Nash challenged Shea. "I'm not sure what you are up to, but she's a nice old lady, so go easy on her."

"Just keeping the customers happy, Pops. No sweat."

"Pops" the others sometimes called Nash, because they were in their mid-twenties, Roland and Mari a bit older, perhaps, and Nash had two decades on them. Mostly, it did not bother Nash, friendly kidding, except that from Shea, it always came out more like a taunt or a challenge. "Old" therefore "weak" therefore "Why the hell should Caitlin choose to bestow her considerable charms on you?"

Nash shrugged off the edge in Shea's comment. He had had his share of trouble when he allowed his temper to get the best of him. Years ago, his father had lectured him that a man could generally get by with either a hot temper or with a taste for drink, but not both. It took a good marriage gone bad and a stint of wearing an orange jumpsuit issued by the county for the lesson to sink in with Nash, but, for the past few years, he had set his mind on bringing both faults into check.

The crew spent the next few hours patching. Shea nailed shingles haphazardly here and there, just trying to find use for the bundles Roland hauled up. Nash handled the legitimate repair the best he could with what was available. Caitlin had sold Mrs. Bellingham twice what she needed, so he could afford to select the best of the lot for his work. He managed a passable job by covering the worst of the leaky sections with new tar paper and undamaged shingles. And he installed some flashing on the peak for protection against rain and snow. *No work of art*, he judged, *but it should get Mrs. Bellingham through a winter or two.*

Later in the afternoon, Caitlin pulled into the driveway. She had been out scouting for any last-minute business before they headed south. The deal was, she collected a down payment or two, "Just to cover material costs," she explained in that tone of voice that could talk the feathers off a duck's back. Invariably, in the rush to move on, the actual repair work was neglected and the net result was a little something to sweeten the travel budget and the self-asserted promise among the crew to "make good when we pass back through."

She and Darcy climbed from the van, and Caitlin called up to Nash and Shea, "Hot today! You boys drink plenty of water."

Darcy waved to Nash, and he asked, "If I got three cookies, and I give your momma one, how many cookies do I have left?"

And Darcy shouted back, "None, 'cause you'll give me the other two!" then she laughed, a deeper laugh than you would expect from a seven-year-old.

Before Nash could respond, Shea interrupted, "Darcy, honey, tell your momma I got a cookie for her too."

Caitlin glanced at Shea with one of those looks that caused Nash's jaw to tighten.

Around three, the skies darkened and a light rain began. Nothing serious, a gentle shower was all, but enough to drive Shea from the roof. Nash followed him down to find Lyle and Roland already dozing in the van. They were to have been prepping the attic and the base-ment, but when the rain began, they had just assumed the crew would be knocking off for the day. Nash took the jug of iced tea from the front porch and knocked on the door but got no answer, so he carried it around back, where he found Darcy just outside the kitchen door eating a peach and practicing in the alphabet booklet he had bought for her a while back. Strings of Ds in large block letters filled two-thirds of a page. He ruffled her hair and opened the back door to the kitchen and set the jug inside. Mrs. Bellingham was at the table shelling beans into a colander.

"Guess we'll be knocking off for the day. Have you seen Caitlin?"

Mrs. Bellingham looked up from her shelling. "I thought she was outside with you."

As Darcy and Nash walked to the truck, they met Caitlin coming out the front door.

"What were you doing in there?" Nash asked.

"Just poking around. Let's go."

That evening, back at the motel, the crew sat outside their rooms in plastic chairs protected by the overhang. The soft rain fell straight down and cooled the day. They drank beer and watched small puddles form in the hard-packed dirt of the parking lot. The talk was easy and of little consequence, and Nash paid no attention, until he picked up a snatch of something from Shea.

" … And those fields, damn sure she's worth a bundle. Bet she's got a stash right there in the house too."

"More than she could ever spend," Lyle agreed.

"That's ignorant talk," Nash interrupted. "Most of

these country folks live hand to mouth."

"Easy, Pops," Shea said. "I'm just speculating a bit. Just passing time." He shook a cigarette from a pack rolled in his sleeve and lit it.

Nash felt the beer working up through his blood. "That 'Pops' business is wearing a little thin."

They eyed one another in the edgy silence. The smoke from Shea's cigarette drifted up between them. Roland busied himself peeling the label from his bottle, and Mari seemed to be trying to decipher some hidden code in the flash of the neon Vacancy sign over by the office.

"Lighten up, boys." Caitlin placed her hand on Nash's knee but looked at Shea. "Can't afford to pay the motel for broken furniture."

Nash rose and joined Darcy inside, where she was watching a show about humpbacked whales and coloring in her book. He could hear the others outside resume their talking, voices rising and falling as night came on, laughing occasionally.

When darkness fell, Caitlin ducked inside to brush her hair and reapply some lipstick. "Think we'll run over to that club. I hear there's a band. Want to come?"

Nash stood at the bathroom door, studying her reflection in the mirror as she traced a fine line on her upper eyelids. Her eyes shone with the effect of a few beers, and as the makeup went on, Nash sensed a change in her, a sexual power beginning to exude from her and fill the room like a perfume. Nash caught her eye in the mirror and motioned to Darcy, who sat cross-legged by the television.

Caitlin looked at him dismissively and called over to her daughter, "If we run out for an hour or two, you'll be okay watching TV, won't you, baby?"

"Sure, Momma."

"I don't feel much like going out," Nash said.

"Suit yourself."

Caitlin dug into her purse and retrieved a thin gold necklace that she latched around her neck.

"I've not seen that before," Nash commented. "Where'd you come by it?"

"Must've been buried in my bag. Noticed it just this moment."

Hours later, Darcy long asleep, Nash heard the van and the truck squeal into the parking lot, then a boisterous exchange, and he looked out the window to watch the crew drift to their rooms, and things quieted back down. But Caitlin and Shea remained in the pickup, talking low. Caitlin rested her back against the passenger door with her legs up on the front seat, looking at Shea through the opening in her bent knees. Something about them bothered Nash, maybe their easy familiarity and the way Shea's body angled toward Caitlin, hovering, predatory. Later, when she climbed into bed, Nash kept turned from her, and she did not seem to notice.

He lay awake, wondering how he had gotten caught up in this life. The others, being young, saw the road paved with opportunity for easy scores. Nash saw only shady deals and a train wreck waiting just around the next bend.

▸ ▸ ▸

He had met Caitlin in a roadhouse outside Greeley two years ago when he was deep into a losing streak, out of work and out of love. Caitlin offered him a chance at both. She needed someone who knew his way around a hammer and nail, and Nash needed to be needed. More than once, he had tried to call it quits, but the curl of Caitlin's body had grown addictive.

Besides, there was Darcy to think of. Nash had taken to the child, and she to him. She was impish, full of curiosity, and bright as a new penny. Nash worried that without him around, the only nourishment for her growing mind would come from the television that seemed to be constantly blaring. Caitlin had been only a child herself when she bore Darcy and, to Nash's observation, lacked the instinct for motherhood. Darcy and Caitlin acted like best friends around one another, on equal footing, playing, giggling, and bickering.

Caitlin and he shared no home other than the road, and that seemed to Nash a sandy foundation on which to build a future. In and out of motels and vans all through the flood and tornado season. During the dog days of summer, Caitlin visited kin down in Texas. For one reason or another, Nash had not been invited either of the past two summers, so he wandered back to Colorado, where he had people in the ground he liked to pay respect to now and again, and occasionally he felt compelled to dredge up some old memories and roll them around in his mind while hiking in the mountains.

When they met back up in late August to chase the fall weather, Caitlin would be full of new plans and Darcy would dance with excitement to see Nash again. Beginning of this season, he had bought her a present of pink sneakers—two sizes too large, it turned out, yet she wore them constantly, refusing even to remove them for bed. She had almost grown into them.

▶ ▶ ▶

Nash did not think he had slept at all, but he found himself waking to the sound of rain pinging against the window. He ran out to buy coffee, milk for Darcy, a few egg sandwiches, and when he returned, Caitlin and Darcy were awake. Caitlin worked the remote, switching between the weather channel and one of those daytime talk shows where the next person was more screwed up than the last, where some guy's transsexual lover was cheating on him with his own son, that kind of thing.

Darcy looked up from the television when Nash entered. "Nash, is that person a man or a lady?"

"Well, Darcy, I'd say maybe a little of both." Nash tried to remember whether he had seen a playground around town. The rain was easing, after all.

"I don't think you can be a boy and a girl both. Does that person have a weenie or not?"

"I bet this place has a library. Let's go see," Nash answered, but before he could grab Darcy's plastic raincoat, Caitlin came up with another idea.

"I need Darcy to help me poke around."

Lately, Caitlin had decided Darcy was old enough to begin learning the business.

"Why don't you go on while Darcy and I check out a book?" Nash countered, knowing the answer ahead of time.

"I need you to get the crew moving. Need to finish up with Mrs. Bellingham. Darcy and I will be along later."

"Darcy, honey, run over to Mari's and see if they're ready to go, will you?"

"But, Nash, the show."

"Go ahead. I bet Mari's got the same show on."

After Darcy left, Nash turned to Caitlin. "I don't think you should be using Darcy like this."

"She's cute; the customers like her. Plus, it's time she

got a taste of how things work."

"No, it's time—past time—she put down in one place for a while, settled at one school."

"She goes to school."

"A month here, a month there, that's not proper schooling."

"You read to her, teach her things," Caitlin argued. "You've heard of homeschooling. Think of her as home-schooled."

"It's not fair to her. She's a bright kid."

"What's not fair is for me to be stuck in some dog-shit town making four-fifty an hour plus tips. Living in some third-floor walk-up. I'm going good now, and in another couple of years, I could be set. So drop it, Nash."

"You'd have me to help out. You wouldn't be going it alone."

"I said drop it."

Outside, the rain had tailed off. Caitlin collected Darcy from Mari's room, and they pulled away in one of the vans as Nash began knocking on the others' doors.

At the Bellingham place, Shea seemed more lively than usual. He even helped finish up the roof, and he followed Nash into the attic without being asked. His behavior put Nash on guard.

They began replacing attic insulation that had some water damage from the last big storm. Only a small corner of the attic was drenched, but Caitlin and Mari had convinced Mrs. Bellingham to replace the insulation entirely. Nash did not know where Roland had dug up the fiberfill, but it was neither up to code nor anywhere near the R-factor advertised to Mrs. Bellingham. Shea had been ferrying up the rolls while Nash laid it out, but when Shea was slow returning from downstairs, Nash peeked out of the dormer window and spotted him and Caitlin walking down the drive, heads together in private conversation. They both seemed animated, and Caitlin pointed to the house and then to Shea like she was explaining something to him. Shea returned to the house, but Nash did not hear his footsteps on the stairs. When he required another roll of insulation, he climbed down from the attic and ran into Caitlin out by the pickup.

"I sent Shea to round up the rest. We need to wrap things up, Nash."

"Not half finished with the attic, and Roland and Lyle are just starting the patch work in the basement."

"Just haul the insulation to the attic and leave it. We've already been paid."

Caitlin looked to the south, toward the Louisiana line, Nash imagined. She appeared excited and on edge.

She turned to him. "Darcy and I got a little something to finish up yet in the house. I need you to take the others and head down the road. Pull off at that rest stop south of

Owensboro and wait for us."

"I don't know what you got planned, but I don't like the feel of it."

Caitlin closed the distance between them and caressed Nash's chest with her open palm. "You worry too much. You need to relax." She moved two fingers between the buttons on his shirt and played with the hair on his chest. "I got plans to set us up. Just let me take care of business."

"Leave Darcy out of this," Nash said.

"I need her to visit a while with Mrs. Bellingham." Caitlin's voice had turned sharp as flint. "Now get the others and do as I say."

Caitlin started for the house, and Nash grabbed her arm. "Wait—"

She spun around and slapped him hard across the face. "Never lay hold of me like that!" she spat.

Nash let his arm fall to his side.

"Let me ask you something," she said, eyes burning into him. "Do you know who Darcy's father is?"

"I do not."

"Well, neither do I. Could be one of a half-dozen men. Hell, a dozen. But I'm out from under that life now. I'm on my own. Free. I call the shots, and nobody, not you, not nobody, is going to turn me back."

Caitlin stomped into the house, and Nash stood by the truck, waiting for the red to clear from his vision. He was planted there, one hand gripping the truck's door handle and the other opening and closing into a tight fist. His mind did not register the passage of time. He may have heard Roland call to him as the others left in one of the vans, but he did not respond. He remained glued in place, and to a casual observer, he would appear a statue, but his mind raced, teetering back and forth on the edge of decision.

A rough push to his shoulder roused him from his trance. He turned to face Shea, who was red-faced and jumpy with adrenaline. Nash wondered if he might be hopped up on something.

"Jesus, Pops, what are you still doing here? The others took the van, right?"

"I don't know."

"Well, shit. You're supposed to be out of here. Now get your ass moving."

Nash started toward the house.

"Not in there!" Shea shouted.

And again Nash felt a hand on his shoulder spin him around, and this time he turned with the momentum and swung hard into Shea's solar plexus and saw his breath catch in his throat, his mouth working into a round oval, lips pursed, trying to suck air like a fish thrown onto the riverbank. That old darkness overcame Nash, the one he thought he had gotten the best of, and his eyes went blank, his mind short-circuited, and his fists pumped, independent of any conscious intent. When Shea doubled over, Nash stepped forward to bring his knee up into Shea's face, but he hesitated, some vestige of self-control reining him in, counterbalancing his rage, and in that hesitation, there was a flash of movement, and Nash felt a sharp pain in his thigh. He jumped back to regroup as Shea came up with a knife and slashed wildly. Nash dodged out of arms' reach and could tell that Shea had neither the will nor the strength to press the attack, so he held his ground. Shea feigned a charge, then broke away and disappeared around the side of the house.

Hobbled by the gash in his leg, Nash ran as best as he could into the house, through the living room, and into the kitchen. Darcy sat with Mrs. Bellingham watching a small television perched at one end of the table.

Darcy looked up when he entered. "I like Oprah, Nash. She has a smiley face."

"Let's go."

"I can't, Nash. I have to sit right here and keep Mrs. Bellingham company."

"I told Caitlin I'd watch the girl for a few minutes," Mrs. Bellingham concurred. "Something about an errand."

"There is danger about. You'd best come with us."

"I'll do no such."

"Then call 911 and get to the basement. I have no

time to explain."

Nash pulled Darcy from the kitchen as she struggled against him.

"Nash, I can't leave." The girl pulled away. "You'll ruin everything. Caitlin gave me a big job to do."

Nash froze. *Caitlin*, she had called her, not *momma*. A line crossed, a partnership sealed. "You're coming with me."

"No, stop!" Darcy cried, and suddenly Caitlin appeared from the back hallway, charging at Nash.

He caught her by the throat and pinned her against the wall, holding her there, tightening his grip, until the anger in her eyes turned to fear, then panic, and he continued to squeeze. Somewhere far off, his mind registered the sound of Mrs. Bellingham calling into a telephone and of Darcy screaming, until finally the pelting of her fists against his injured thigh brought him back from where he had been, and he loosened his hold on Caitlin's throat. She slumped to her knees. Darcy draped herself over her mother, but Nash pried her away and tucked her under his arm and stalked to the front door. As he reached for the knob, he felt a dull thump between his shoulder blades. The thought of Shea and the knife flashed through his mind, and he instinctively swung behind him with a backhand. He pivoted in time to see a broom skittering across the foyer and Mrs. Bellingham's head slapping the hardwood floor with a crack like a rifle shot.

Nash stood above them, stunned, Caitlin still on her knees, gasping for breath, Mrs. Bellingham motionless at his feet, the room gone still but for Darcy's whimpers and the sound of *Oprah* drifting in from the kitchen television. He felt the heat draining like blood from his body. Shivering at the cold reality of their lives, the futility of even attempting to make things right, Nash gently set Darcy down, and, before leaving, he walked to the kitchen, where he made a quick call to 911 and turned off the television.

▶ ▶ ▶

Near sunset, mist filtered through low clouds as Nash guided the pickup westward. The land appeared dusky in the waning light, the fields rank with crops too wet to harvest, the air pungent with the scent of loss. He drove on, thinking briefly of Caitlin. They would be in southern Kentucky, Caitlin behind the wheel, Shea with an ice bag to his face, Darcy asleep between them. Caitlin would have considered giving chase—Nash had taken her pickup—but then her mind would have focused on the weather brewing in Louisiana, the wealth of opportunities bequeathed by the storm, and she would keep her van pointed south.

Caitlin always looked ahead, he thought, *to the next town, to the next storm.*

▶ *Gary Schanbacher*

28

She would give little concern to who might be in pursuit, even less to the fate of Mrs. Bellingham. Those worries were left to Nash, and he felt their weight trying to bury him, but he refused to allow it. Instead, he concentrated on the odometer, watching the slow tick of miles accumulate on the meter. He turned off the wipers until mist coated the windshield. His world compressed around him, condensed into this moment in this truck. The mist blurred his vision of the road ahead, helped obscure the memory of what had been left behind, and for a while he was able to forget the truth about himself as he drove on into the shadowy future.

A Garden in Drought

Mid-July, ninety-seven degrees. Alvin worked in his garden, staking tomatoes with bamboo rods and green plastic tape. As he bent over the plants, sweat dripped from his nose onto the dull-green leaf of an 'Early Girl.' He stood to mop his face with a rag, the soft remnants of an old cotton sock. In the yard west of him, he noticed his neighbor watching him from a multicolored lawn chair under the back porch awning. He wore a garish orange T-shirt stretched to its limit by a gut that forced him into a splayed-legged slump. Strangeway's son, Alvin recognized. The boy had inherited the house following the old man's death that spring. The elder had been an altogether disagreeable character, and the acorn had fallen close to the tree, as best Alvin could tell.

Junior called over to him, "Don't know why you're wasting time with those things. Nothing will come of them."

Alvin looked over at Junior without acknowledging him. He thought about the words that had drifted across the yards, syrupy slow in the heat, then spat on the ground.

Alvin had worked hard his entire life, drawing a paycheck until after his seventy-fourth birthday—foreman of a road-paving crew, concrete finisher, manager of a building-supply warehouse ... he did not suffer fools or sluggards lightly, and this one appeared close kin to both.

Alvin chose to remain silent and went back to his staking.

Junior struggled out of the lawn chair and shuffled over. Resting his meaty forearms on the fence, he studied Alvin for a bit. "I said," Junior talked loudly and slowly, "seems like a waste of energy. Nothing will grow in this goddamn heat."

Alvin plucked a radish and held it out to Junior. "Already got me a crop of sorts."

He occupied himself with his sweat rag while Junior wiped dirt from the root using his T-shirt, popped it into his mouth, chewed thoughtfully for a second, then puckered up and hacked out bits of red-and-white confetti. "Holy shit, that thing's hotter'n a Tijuana whore!"

Alvin chuckled as Junior hurried back to his house, rump pumping up and down like two enormous hams bouncing in a sack. He returned to his work.

It had been a trying summer, since rain had abandoned the land altogether by June. The tomatoes came up spindly and showed signs of heat stress. He had taken to misting them with a spray bottle during the heat of the day, and gradually they responded, inching upward, eking out a sprinkling of blossoms. By early July, a few green fruits had set—small as wrens' eggs, and not many at that, but enough. Enough to keep Alvin going.

The vines were weak from drought and needed staking, so Alvin worked through midday while the sun continued throwing its heat, and eventually Alvin felt himself going weak-kneed and clammy. He stumbled in a drunkard's weave back inside the house, where he splashed his face with tap water, unfastened his overalls, and loosened the buttons on his shirt. He made it to the couch and flopped down. That is where his daughter, Elaine, found him.

"Dad? For heaven's sake, look at what your boots have done to the upholstery."

Alvin awoke as his feet were being lifted from the sofa. For a moment, he could not locate himself, thought he was still out in the garden. He took the white of the ceiling for the white light beating down on him. He sat up and felt around for his roll of green tape. "Must've fallen out of my pocket," he said.

Elaine stood above him. "What on earth are you talking about? Were you asleep? You never sleep in the daytime. When did you start napping?"

"I am eighty-four years old. I have a right to nap when I damn well please."

"And cursing—when did you take up cursing? Dad, you're not yourself lately."

Still sitting groggily on the couch, Alvin became vexed at having to crane up at his daughter standing over him, so he struggled to his feet, only to find himself sprawled on the floor, black dots flying about the room, a female voice modulating in and out of his consciousness. After a little while, the shadows began taking on definition again, hazy lines sharpened, the living room slowed its spinning.

His daughter leaned over him and pressed a palm to his forehead. "Dad, are you okay?" she asked, her voice softening. "You've overdone it again in that garden of yours, haven't you? I asked you not to plant this year. I can't be here all the time to watch over you."

"Thank the almighty God," Alvin tried to say, but the words remained floating in thought.

Not to plant. What a thought. He had cultivated a garden for as many years past as his memory carried— bush beans, peppers, spring onions, melons, tomatoes. The tomatoes were especially dear to him: the 'Early Girls,' 'Big Boys,' 'Brandywines.' As a child, he had helped in the family plot, a quarter acre of black dirt, rich and bountiful for a poor family. And later, after the war, out behind the small pillbox of a house he had bought for his wife and small children, he had dug a small pocket garden and planted carrots and sweet peas. As the years passed, he had expanded the garden, and now it filled nearly the entire backyard. Not plant? Nonsense.

"Do you feel faint?" Elaine asked. "Flushed? At the assisted-living center, they'd know how to help."

It had begun last winter, Elaine's increasingly strident appeals. There had been a fall on the ice, a broken hip, a week in the hospital, and another two in a short-term rehabilitation facility. Alvin swore never to set foot in such a place again.

"They said if the mailman hadn't been running late because of the storm, you would have frozen to death right there in your front yard."

"And not a bad way to go," Alvin had countered. "I'd have chosen that as the lesser of two evils if I'd known what was waiting for me."

The pain he could abide, but the feeling of utter dependence and the medication-induced dullness he could not.

It was during his convalescence at home that Elaine began ordering brochures through the mail and stopping by with information packets on "senior-choice" apartments and "carefree-living" centers. Alvin accumulated them on the table, and every several days, he threw out the bottom half and added the new arrivals to the stack. After weeks of ignoring Elaine's petitions, Alvin began receiving thin envelopes in the mail from a legal firm. He added them, unread, to the pile too.

"We just need to see about getting your affairs in order," Elaine said about the notes from the attorney, and Alvin wondered exactly who "we" might be. There was only Elaine and his boy, Nash, whom he had not heard from in a long while.

"You need to face the future," Elaine said, "and it's my responsibility to see to it you're looked after."

"It is your responsibility to leave well enough alone."

▶ ▶ ▶

Now, slumped on the living room floor, Alvin felt her words nipping at him, and he determined to resist her line of reasoning. But when he tried groping to his feet, the room dissolved once again, and he sensed a gray fog descending upon him like wood smoke settling into a valley.

When he next became fully conscious of his surroundings, the room had been transformed. A ladder-back chair and a small wooden table had replaced his wife's armchair with its lace antimacassars. He noticed that he was wearing a blue gown, like one of his old nightshirts, except open-assed, and he vaguely remembered being slipped into it by two sets of strong female hands. The room smelled of disinfectant and of a familiar food—chicken-noodle soup? He sat up in bed, a strange bed with the top sheet and coverlet tucked securely under the mattress, unrumpled, as if he had been slipped beneath them with care not to wrinkle anything. The window showed weak light—dusk or dawn, he could not tell. With effort, he stripped off his covers and got slowly to his feet. His balance felt sure, though his head throbbed slightly. He found his clothes, dressed, walked into the hall, and made for an Exit sign.

A woman dressed in a white uniform hurried up beside him. "You shouldn't be out of bed. Let me help you back. I was just bringing you this meal form to fill out—no diet restrictions. You have choices."

"Yes, I do," Alvin answered, without slowing his march. "Won't be staying for supper."

The lady tried to continue. "You were brought in here dehydrated and disoriented. You really need to wait for the doctor to follow up with you."

But Alvin ignored her completely, refusing to hear a word she said. He opened an exit door, stepped outside, and closed the door firmly behind him.

Alvin noted the pale glow on the western horizon. Evening. He must have passed the afternoon in that place. He did not know the neighborhood, what with all the renovation and infilling going on these days in the city, but he guessed he must be somewhere north of his home, so he set his course and began walking with purpose.

He hiked south for a dozen blocks, but the streets remained vaguely unfamiliar to him—and this in a city he had called his own for the best part of a century. After a while, his pace slowed, and he turned and began retracing his steps. Then, disoriented, he turned around again, pushed on for a bit, then sat down on a bus-stop bench, massaged his temples, and tried to remember just why he came to be walking in the first place.

Dark began to fall. A bus pulled up to the curb, and the driver asked Alvin what route he needed. The voice from the bus jolted Alvin to his senses, and he explained where he was headed, and the bus driver brought him on board and helped him with correct change. During the ride home, a shiver of fear overcame Alvin—fear not that he had become lost, but that he had become confused, unaware, unsure of the who and the what and the why of his being.

When he walked into his house, Alvin startled Elaine, who was in his bedroom packing his old duffel with clothes. "My Lord, what are you doing here?"

"Best of my remembrance, I live here."

"But you should be in the hospital. You need rest. I was just about to bring you some things."

"It did take me some time to find my way home. As

for rest, if you could find your own way out, I do believe I could shut my eyelids for a spell."

Elaine put a folded shirt into the bag. "Dad, we've got to talk. You have to listen to reason. It's time for you to let others care for you. You could fall again, you could faint in the heat, and I may not be here to help you next time."

"And … ?" Alvin asked. "So what? What do you suppose the future holds for me? Old men die, that's what. And I aim to die right here in my own house. Sooner or later, can't say. Sorry if it ain't convenient for you, but that's the way it's going to be."

Alvin shooed her from the room with a wave of his hands. But once she had left, his wave became a tremble, and the tremble that began in his hands worked its way through his entire body, and it was all he could manage to make it to bed and wait for a long and restless night to pass.

He knew he was not long for the world; he could inventory time's ravages in the mirror every morning: loose, superfluous folds hanging from his face and waist, sunken chest with breasts that drooped like empty purses, skeletal hands, knuckles swollen like popcorn. His skin seemed to be thinning, barely able to hold together the package of bones and blue veins that remained of his once-sturdy frame. Something had been going wrong with him on the inside during the months since his fall—a sharp pain here, blood there, nothing he cared to see a doctor about. He had lived a long while, and he harbored no grudge against old age. He understood the fullness of time that eroded mountains, pulled stars from the sky, decayed flesh. Some days, he viewed his reflection in the mirror with the objectivity of a judge and thought, *So this is what it's come to*, and he would laugh out loud. His mind remained sharp most of the time, and he was thankful for that double-edged gift—though there were few he cared to share his thoughts with.

The family was gone now, his wife eight years dead, and, in truth, not mourned as deeply as some might expect given a marriage of six decades. Not that there had not been genuine tenderness between them, but they had grown silent those last years, covered pretty much all there was to cover between two people, and rather than repeat themselves, they had just let it go. The boy, Nash, was involved in some kind of itinerant construction work that kept him on the road and unstable in marriage. And the girl, Elaine, was busy with her own family, children and now grandchildren. She called twice a week and popped in unannounced whenever the spirit moved, with the primary motivation, in Alvin's mind, to press him for what remained of his freedom.

▶ ▶ ▶

August. The heat dry, the air static, and everything—the trees, the creatures—quiet and motionless, as if the Earth had stilled its rotation and all life had come to a pause. The fruit was slow to ripen. Alvin could not fight off a deepening anxiety as he inspected his tomatoes each morning for signs of infestation. He worried about hornworms, rot, and blight. He refused to pick any green tomatoes, though in past years, in years of abundant harvest, there would have been green-tomato relish, fried green tomatoes, green-tomato pie. The fruits were too dear this season, and Alvin intended to pick them only when fully vine ripened.

But the waiting proved a strain. He slept only in fits and starts. He rose early each day and made coffee and sat looking out the kitchen window as morning took shape. It seemed to evolve from the shadows of night: first the lighter, straw-colored shades of the parched yard, then individual branches and leaves appeared from the murky ovals of the trees.

And his garden … the bush beans already wasted and collapsed into heaps of brown and brittle foliage. The barren cantaloupe vines, here and there the withered shell of a fruit turned to leather. Only the tomatoes stood upright—stunted and meager of fruit, and only slowly turning in color, but standing and turning nonetheless.

▶ ▶ ▶

Thursday, the first week in September, Alvin finally noticed a few tomatoes over by the back fence that were deep red and beginning to soften. Still, he held off the temptation to pick. He would not be rushed now that they were so close to perfect. He would not be cheated. *Saturday*, he judged. *Saturday would be the day.*

But Saturday, the ripe tomatoes were gone when Alvin went to pick them. Gone. He searched nearby vines lest his memory had failed from just the few days earlier, but he knew it had not. He bent close to the ground and inspected for animal tracks. He carefully lifted the lower vines to check whether the fruit might have already dropped. Nothing. He unbent himself and cussed under his breath. *Wishing won't bring them back*, he thought to himself, and he turned to the rest of his crop, the watering and the weeding. Several more tomatoes would be ready tomorrow.

On Sunday, the garden again refused to give him its produce. All the harvest-ready tomatoes had gone missing. Alvin stood leaning against his hoe, silent and unmoving as a scarecrow, feeling old in the oppressive heat.

"You okay over there?"

Alvin turned to find Junior walking toward him.

Junior squinted in the bright light, appraising the tomato plants. "Well, it does appear that you got your-self something from those sorry-looking vines. Those tomatoes there must be the toughest sons of bitches in the world. Hope for your sake they don't taste like your radishes."

"I wouldn't know how they taste. Seems the ripe ones grow legs and walk off before I can get to them."

"Oh, I suppose there's all kind of varmints that would take a interest in your crop. Raccoons, skunks, squirrels."

"Well, you are correct," Alvin said as he began walking back to the house. "I do suspect a varmint."

Alvin rested on and off Sunday afternoon. He felt out of sorts, light headed. When evening came on, he drank a beer by the kitchen window as the daylight faded. He turned off all the house lights and pushed a chair close by the window. With a nearly full moon, he could watch the garden for movement. He sat like that for hours, occasionally dozing off, only to awaken with a start and scold himself for being old and weak willed.

Deep into the night, a fox traversed the yard, passing through the garden and jumping the back fence and fading into the background. Once, near morning, a dark shadow swooped down from the sky and glided low to the ground and disappeared again into the black. An owl?

Alvin was not conscious of daylight coming on; perhaps he had slept again. He pulled himself stiffly out of the chair and walked outside. To the best of his telling, the garden had not been violated during the night. He returned to the house and made himself coffee and eggs and two pieces of toast. The breakfast set well with him, but afterward he felt an overwhelming weariness and decided to rest for a bit before again taking up his vigil. Several of the tomatoes were skin-splitting ripe, and he knew that sometime today he would find out who or what was thieving from him.

But first, he would rest. Lying down on top of his bedcovers, he listened to the interrupted silence of the house, the creaking of a joist, the intermittent hum of the refrigerator motor kicking on. Just before nodding off, he thought of his wife, how their self-imposed silence seemed so much richer than the silence of his life now. He thought of his son, Nash, full of the same restless energy that had driven Alvin to the garden year after year and Nash away from home as soon as he was able to fend for himself, at seventeen. And Elaine, never sure how she fit in, never sure where she stood in a family unable to articulate their expectations, the distinction between approval or reproach often conveyed by the slightest angle of the chin, the subtlest of gestures, a tentative offer of a hand, a clenching and unclenching of the fist while gazing off into the distance. He understood the burden he had imposed on his children by his reticence, and for that, he felt remorse.

Alvin awoke in the early afternoon, upset for sleeping so long, but during sleep a plan had come to him. He rose, went outside, and watered his garden, checking for loss and finding none. He returned to the kitchen and searched through the pantry for one of his wife's rolling pins. He considered its heft with satisfaction and remembered several years back when one of the grandkids, Elaine's oldest girl perhaps, had come upon it and had no idea what such an implement might be. Elaine had little success explaining the process by which flour was turned into dough and then into biscuits or piecrust, in part because she herself had such limited experience upon which to draw. He set the rolling pin on a kitchen chair and waited for nightfall.

▶ ▶ ▶

Full dark. Outside in his garden, kitchen chair wedged into the corner of the fence, rolling pin across his knees, Alvin waited. It had been a trying season, he had worked hard, and he would brook no quarter with vegetable thieves, man or beast, especially given the prospect of so meager a crop. He dozed off and on and dreamt of tomatoes—more than that, a memory: growing up poor. Hazy recollections of hard times in the thirties. Jobs scarce, newspaper photos of men wearing fedoras and silk ties and loitering in soup lines.

His father clung to part-time work at a butcher shop,

and each evening he gave thanks for the offal, the beef gristle, the chicken gizzards he was able to scavenge for the table. If the garden yielded tomatoes, their simple meals were enhanced, given flavor: macaroni with tomatoes his mother had put up the autumn before; tart chutney to slop onto the meat trimmings; in season, fresh red slabs dusted with salt and pepper. Out of their abundance, his mother set out green-tomato pies on the back porch for the jobless men who had abandoned home to wander the forlorn cities searching for work. Too proud to ask for handouts, they would take the pies and leave a token payment: a button, a tie tack. For Alvin's family, the garden allowed for self-sufficiency—and more: charity.

The sound of a door creaking open made Alvin jerk his chin up from where it had settled onto his chest. A weak light shone from Junior's back door, and the bulk of his shadow moved toward the garden. He stumbled once, as if his eyes had yet to adjust to the darkness. He approached the fence, so close Alvin could smell the odor of alcohol coming off his body. Junior put his hands to his lower back, arched his upper body, looked up into the heavens, and swayed like a tree in variable wind. Then he bent slightly at the waist, steadied himself by placing his outstretched arm on Alvin's fence, unzipped his jeans, and began urinating loudly into Alvin's garden. He let pass a great bellowing wind and belched. Alvin sat there watching the desecration of his garden for as long as he could take it—only a few seconds—then stood, summoned his strength, the accumulated dregs of energy remaining from seven decades of hard labor, raised the rolling pin above his head, and swung it down onto Junior's arm. They both grunted in unison, one from exertion and the other from pain. Alvin let the rolling pin drop and slumped back into his chair, legs suddenly gone as spindly and weak as his drought-withered vines. Junior moaned a low animal-like sound and staggered off, with his arm dangling by his side.

Halfway to his door, he turned and screamed back into the dark, "Son of a bitch! You're one crazy son of a bitch!"

"You leave be my tomatoes! You leave them be!"

"What do I want with your tomatoes, old man? I'm calling the cops!"

Junior disappeared into his house, and Alvin remained sitting. Disoriented, laboring for breath, his heart pounded at an almost unbearable rate.

Gradually, the veil lifted from his eyes, as if he had passed through the shadow of the valley of death and, this time, emerged from it yet in this world. He stood, gripping the fence rail, testing his legs. He found them untrustworthy, so he sat back down. He would rest a while. Even though he had yet to solve the mystery of his disappearing tomatoes, he wanted now only the comfort of his bed. He would regain his strength and then make his way back inside.

The night wore on—the moon sank below the horizon, the heat of the day dissipated, and again Alvin dozed. He awoke in the dreamy half-light and looked around in confusion. He sat in the silence, taking in the gathering dawn.

Then, out of the corner of his eye, he caught movement, a shadow creeping across the back lawn. Into the garden, moving cautiously, was a shape like that of a humpbacked cat. He recognized a raccoon sneaking its way into the center of his vision. It sniffed the tomatoes and tested one, then another in its forepaws, finally settling on one, picking it, daintily eating.

Alvin watched the raccoon eat the tomato. Nature's product to nature's product, a necessary balance. Alvin could appreciate the trade.

But when it reached for another tomato, Alvin took up the rolling pin and challenged the animal. "Enough," he said. "You've had your share."

The startled raccoon backed out of the garden, hissing and showing its teeth, then disappeared over the back fence.

Alvin set the rolling pin against the fence and reached over to pick the object of the raccoon's desire, a fully ripened 'Brandywine' of improbable size, given the season's growing conditions. He admired its wholeness, round and balanced. When he brought the tomato to his lips, it was as if the skin had been waiting a lifetime for his touch. His mouth filled with pulp, the nostalgic sweetness of summer itself. Of life. Juice dribbled from his chin onto his shirtfront. Alvin sat there on a kitchen chair in the corner of his garden, rolling pin at his feet, sat there in that quiet new dawning of yet another day, and savored his harvest.

A Father's Peace

As the Kansas plains stretched out before him, Nash felt relieved to be done with the East, where heavy air lowered the sky and thick stands of trees drew in the horizon. One foreign to this land might see only a flat wasteland, dry as straw, barren of life; Nash knew better. The prairie supported—if meagerly—a collection of living things: a dozen stave-sided cattle nosing a mud hole, a coyote stalking mice through the windbreaks, a red-tailed hawk casting a shadow over the tawny grasses. Life was inconspicuous here, blended into the land.

It was a rain-starved time, and Nash drove past section after section left fallow, the monotony broken here and there by fields of sunflowers. When he crossed over into Colorado, even the sunflowers forsook the land.

Still, he continued west, nearer to his past, and deep into the day, the mountains came into view, blue in the distance, rising from the plains like a barrier at the end

▸

of the world. Nash pulled off the interstate northeast of Denver and traversed the back roads, past new housing developments growing in neat rows from fields that had once held winter wheat.

His old neighborhood was wedged into the northern edge of the city, a square of residential space carved from the gritty industrial districts that employed its working-class residents. On a side street, Nash parked beside a modest frame house with white siding. He switched off the ignition and sat in the truck looking off to the west, where virga streamed from thunderheads rolling along the Front Range. The afternoon sun illuminated the cloud caps so they shone radiant white. After a while, he climbed from the truck and followed the concrete walk to the front porch. When no one answered his rap at the door, he tried the knob, found it locked, and went around to the side yard. He peered into the windows—no movement, no clutter inside. In the backyard, he noticed bindweed threading the chain links of the fence and bull thistle in the garden growing almost as tall as the stunted tomato plants. It was unlike his father to let the garden go untended.

"Looking for the old man? Alvin Padgett?"

Nash turned. A fat man with his right arm in a sling stood by the side fence. A baseball cap sat back on his head, and his hair stood out at the sides like wings.

"I am."

"Won't find him here. They hauled him away a few weeks back. Stuck him in a old folks home."

Nash picked up a clod of dirt and tossed it without malicious intent toward a magpie pecking for insects in the brown grass. "What for?"

"That is one crazy old son of a bitch. Took a bat to me," the fat man said and held out his injured arm in evidence. "I'd sue him if I thought he had a dime."

"Yeah, I suppose you would," Nash said.

The man stepped back from the fence. Nash had a deeply lined face that evoked caution when it turned hard.

Far in the distance, a slow roll of thunder sounded a hollow promise of rain that no one in this part of the country any longer believed.

Nash returned to the truck and drove past Angelica's place but did not stop, because of Roy's squad car parked in her driveway.

The house looked little changed from when last he had seen it, two years earlier, yet something about it seemed entirely foreign to him. He felt no part of it at all, even though he and Angelica, and, later, Robbie, had made a life here for the better part of a decade. Only after he rounded the block and passed by for a second time did it register that Robbie's swing set was missing from the corner of the backyard. Robbie had loved that swing set.

Nash had a vision of Robbie's hands curled around the rope, of him begging Nash, "Higher, higher … " A scene from a better time.

Robbie had been coming to Nash lately in his dreams. Robbie is playing in the yard while Anjelica starts dinner in the kitchen. When Nash comes home from work, he can smell the sweetness of sautéing peppers and onions drifting through the house. He kisses Angelica and tastes the pepper she had sampled and then grabs a beer on his way outside. Robbie jumps with excitement to see him and runs to the swing.

Nash did not remember whether any of this had actually occurred in the past—he imagined it must have—but the absence of the swing set in the backyard somehow made the dream less real in his mind, and he felt a little cheated.

He stopped the truck in the street and studied the vacant patch of lawn, feeling a vacancy seep into his body like hunger pangs, and reached for the door handle. But then he thought he noticed a curtain flutter in the front window, and he refocused on Roy's squad car and drove on.

There had been trouble back East in Indiana, and the authorities might be looking for him. If information was floating through the airwaves, Roy would know about it; he was thorough that way. The two had been close when younger, but a wedge of jealousy had come between them when Angelica drifted Nash's way rather than Roy's, and later, after Nash had allowed drink and a short temper to rule his life, it had been Roy who had dogged him.

Nash continued on to his sister's house, and Elaine answered the door before he reached the bell.

"Nash," she said with tenderness, and reached a hand out to touch his arm. It seemed as if the simple physical contact served to channel the sentimentality out of her system, to bring her back to the present, and she dropped her arm to her side and her voice went flat. "What brings you home?"

"Where's Dad? I was out to the house."

"I've had to move him. Where help is close when he needs it."

"It wasn't your place."

"Of course it was. You haven't been around much, remember?"

Elaine stepped aside, and Nash entered her small house. With her kids grown, the front room possessed the depressing neatness of an elderly spinster. Pictures of Elaine's children and grandchildren were arranged on the tables, but there was no evidence that children had ever cluttered the rooms and no sign at all that her husband had spent thirty years there. Cut-glass knickknacks, artificial flowers in a garish vase—the place seemed sterile and arid.

Hanging in the foyer was a picture of their family. In it, he was maybe ten and wore a T-shirt with horizontal stripes like a barber's pole. Nash still remembered that shirt. Alvin posed with his hand resting on Nash's shoulder, appearing uncomfortable in a bow tie. Elaine, already grown, stood beside their mother. They were both attractive if unremarkable: even features, brown shoulder-length hair done up in the permanent wave popular at that time.

"He's not like he used to be," Elaine explained. "Fell last winter, broke a hip. We almost lost him. Mind comes and goes. But still strong and ornery as a billy goat. Got violent with a neighbor."

"I saw that man," Nash said. "A big man. Looked like he should've been able to take care of himself."

"Dad couldn't stay in that house through another winter without someone to keep an eye on him, and since I've had to go back to work, I can't be there all the time. And you've been away."

"I'm here now."

"For how long?"

"Who knows? A while. When can I see him?"

"You can't for now. He's kept to himself since he moved over there, like he's embarrassed. A few of the old guys from work tried to stop by and he would have none of it."

"Well, then."

"You have a place to stay?" Elaine asked.

"My truck."

"Here, take his key. I've not put the old place on the market yet. I'll let him know you're back. Sunday, I'll try to bring him over after church."

As Nash left, Elaine called out to him, "Been to see Angelica yet?"

"I have not."

Then, softer, Elaine asked, "Robbie?"

"No."

Nash returned to his father's house and found a police car parked in front when he pulled up. A patrolman sat on the front porch steps.

Nash killed the engine, climbed from the truck, and moved slowly up the walkway. "Roy," Nash said, hitching a foot onto the front step and resting an arm on the railing.

"Heard you were back, Nash. Figured you'd end up here, at Alvin's."

"Didn't know myself until just a little while ago. Must have radar there between the ears."

They stood in silence, watching some leaves swirl along the ground in the breeze.

Nash wondered how much Roy knew about Indiana. He had joined up with an itinerant road crew that followed the storms, cleaned up after them—trimmed the trees, repaired roofs. Some in the crew had turned to robbery, and when Nash found out, he had stolen one of their trucks and headed back to Colorado. Nothing big-time at all, but he knew that small-town police departments kept track of the traveling operations that cheated their way through their jurisdictions. "Stop by to pay your respects, did you?"

"Visit is purely professional. Just wondering how long you plan on being here?"

"Can't say. Why the interest?"

"Just seems like you and trouble travel as a pair. Like to head anything off before it gets started."

"Appreciate your concern."

Roy stood and hitched his belt and started for his patrol car, but then turned and walked back to Nash. "You been out to see her. Angelica's already long finished with you. You know it. I know it."

"Could be," Nash said.

"Just leave things be," said Roy.

They eyed each other, then Nash climbed the porch steps and went into the house. Roy retraced his steps to his patrol car and squealed the tires as he left.

Time spent in his old home reminded Nash of both the best and the worst of his childhood. The small one-story box was built just after the war to accommodate repatriated soldiers anxious to start families. Elaine had come first, Nash a decade later as a surprise. The house had always seemed too small to hold him—he felt smothered by a family doting over its baby and by the tight quarters. That restlessness had overtaken his life, made him impatient with others, quick to anger, quick with his fists, quick to move on when pressures built up around him. Even now, as an adult, he found himself unsettled from almost the minute he reclaimed his old room, and it occurred to him that his father's vegetable garden, which had been tended to every summer he could remember, might have served as Alvin's own temporary retreat from that same claustrophobia. For the next few days, Nash kept to himself and stayed busy by cleaning and doing yard chores.

▶ ▶ ▶

Sunday noon. Nash had fried some chicken and bought potato salad and a three-bean concoction and set it all out on the small dining table. When he heard a car door shut, he went to the front window and watched his sister and Alvin come up the walk. His father looked like a diminished, more-sunken version of the man Nash had last visited, a year ago. After the accident, when Nash had quit on Angelica, when he could no longer bear to look her in the eye and had just drifted off, wandering from job to job, searching for and finding trouble of a violent and felonious nature, he knew his father had been pained to watch his unraveling. Alvin was a simple man with a straightforward approach to life: you endured, worked hard, persevered; you did not run from your problems, you faced them square-shouldered, head on. As Nash watched his father approach, he wondered how he might be received.

Alvin still limped from the slip on the ice last winter that had broken his hip, and his spine was curved, as if he were trying to fold himself away. But when Nash opened the door, Alvin straightened, pulled free of Elaine's grip on his elbow, marched up the front steps, and clasped his son by the shoulders. Nash was surprised by the strength still remaining in his father's hands.

"You look a little off your feed, boy. You eating right?"

"I'm fine, Dad. How about you?"

"Old," Alvin answered, and went past Nash into his house.

As he walked toward the dining table, Alvin slid his hand across the leather of his armchair in the front room, patted it like a faithful pet, moved on to the table, and sat at his customary place. Nash and Elaine took a chair at either side. Nash passed the plates, and they began to eat.

"Ran into your neighbor the other day," Nash said, pointing his fork in the direction of the side yard.

"Junior Strangeway," Alvin said. "His old man was

never worth a plug nickel, and the son has managed to equal him, with change left over."

"Seems you two had a run in."

"Stealing my tomatoes. Would've gave him as many as he wanted for the asking, but I'll not tolerate a thief."

"He said he had no use at all for your tomatoes," Elaine interrupted.

"Just the same … " Alvin trailed off.

"Says you took a baseball bat to him."

Alvin hooted. "It was one of your mother's old rolling pins. Waited for him in the garden late one night, and when he came out to help himself to my produce, I whacked him a good one. Done him in with a rolling pin." Alvin slapped the table.

Nash chuckled.

"Do we have to have this conversation while we're eating?" Elaine asked. "Can't we talk about something more pleasant?"

"Like how I spend my days in the center?" asked Alvin. "Well, let's see. First, there's the battle about whether or not I need a diaper. Then the discussion about what they call food. Then—"

"Please, Dad," Elaine said. She stood abruptly from the table, almost tipping her chair, and went into the kitchen.

"And recreation!" Alvin hollered after her. "They call sitting us in front of the TV recreation!"

Elaine returned and put a glass of water before Alvin.

"Rather have a beer," he grumbled.

Elaine retook her seat without responding.

The three picked at the food in silence for a bit.

Elaine looked to Nash. "See? He blames me for this. I'm just trying to do what's best."

Alvin studied his potato salad, dissecting it with his fork, as if he were searching for a bug.

"Maybe," Nash started, "we could see about a different arrangement now that I'm back."

"Don't do this," Elaine said. "Don't even start."

"I know you've no cause to trust what I say."

"How long? How long do you intend to stay?"

"I don't know. As long as I need to, I guess."

"A month? Six? A year?"

Nash looked down at his meal and shook his head. He felt a pressure behind his eyes. "Depends. No promises."

"Let's discuss this later," Elaine said as she stood and began clearing the dishes.

"Is there dessert?" Alvin asked. "Pie?"

▶ ▶ ▶

Later that afternoon, Nash again drove to Angelica's place. The streets were quiet. They lived in a part of the country where commerce still slowed on Sunday. Empty streets, quiet storefronts—a melancholy time. But after lunching with Alvin and Elaine, he had felt drawn to complete contact with the important people he had let down, left behind. Roy's squad car was not there, and Nash was grateful for that.

When Angelica answered his ring, something caught in Nash's throat, and for a moment, he could not speak. Much of the radiance that had left Angelica during their last days together had returned, and he discovered himself mute with yearning. So, in the time she allowed, he just looked at her, burned her image into his memory. She had gained some weight, good weight, and her complexion, rich brown, shone, as if illuminated from within. Even with her expression fixed and stern, a kindness escaped from her eyes.

"Hello, Nash." If she was surprised to see him, it did not show.

"Hello, Angelica. Can I come in for a minute?"

"No, I don't think so."

"I understand." Nash put one hand against the door frame and looked off down the tree-lined street. The leaves were just beginning to turn. He looked back at her. "I wanted to see how you were getting along."

"I'm fine."

"I noticed Roy's car in the drive the other day."

"Nash, what did you expect? My life to stop? Well, it did. For a while. Roy's been a friend."

"That's good."

Nash looked at her for a long time, and she did not turn away. There was so much he wished he could tell her, but it never came easy for him, opening up, laying things bare.

"Well," he said, and stepped away from the door.

"Have you been over to see Robbie?" Angelica asked.

"Not yet," Nash said.

"You need to."

"I'm working up to it."

▶ ▶ ▶

Nash did not return straightaway to Alvin's house. Instead, he drove the stolen truck out to the country and parked it off the road in a stand of cottonwoods, then walked back to the state highway and hitched his way into town.

▶ ▶ ▶

Settling in at Alvin's house, Nash spent the next week doing fall cleanup. He gutted the garden of the withered vegetables—bush beans with pods that rattled with shriveled seeds, spiderlike tomato vines, squash plants holding some dried gourds that he set aside in the event Elaine might want them for autumn decorations. He put down slow-release fertilizer on the dry, dormant lawn. Inside, Nash aired the house during the warm September afternoons by opening the windows, and he scrubbed and stripped the kitchen floor and laid down a fresh coat of wax on the ancient linoleum and cleaned the oven of the greasy buildup Alvin had let accumulate over the years. He also looked for work and found a trucking firm that took him on part-time to do local deliveries.

Friday, two weeks after he had returned, Nash came home to find Alvin sitting in his accustomed place, the overstuffed living-room lounger. Sunken into it, he looked like a chick in a nest.

"Dad?"

"Son. What's for dinner?"

"Dad, what are you doing here?"

"We talked the other week, remember? Decided I'd come home."

"I remember the conversation. I don't remember we came to any decision. Did Elaine drive you over here? Does she know you left that place?"

"Best I recall, Elaine is my daughter. I do not believe I need her permission to act as I see fit."

"Dad, there is a right way and a wrong way to go about this. Now, the folks at the home—"

"Folks at the home can kiss my ass. Told them so. I said, 'I'm leaving, and you can kiss my ass.'"

"Well, I guess we've settled on the wrong way. I'll see about supper."

▶ ▶ ▶

The season began turning. Cold came early, but no weather. Alvin busied himself about the garden, planting bulbs along the fence line, turning the soil, and worrying that his garden might not respond next spring to any degree of nurturing.

Nash had fallen into a routine of work and domestic husbandry, but he grew more and more restless. The anniversary he dreaded was once again approaching; the season had changed early then also, coming up on three years ago. The dreams of Robbie recurred most nights, and one morning he awoke with the resolve to visit his son. But he found chores to delay his leaving, and by afternoon the clouds came down from the mountains, low and threatening. The temperature plummeted. Alvin became animated at the prospect of an early snow and pulled Nash outside with him.

"Smell it?" he asked Nash as they toured the yard, Nash in a heavy jacket, Alvin dressed only in a flannel shirt and baggy chinos held up with suspenders. Around the yard he circled, sniffing the air like a hound and nodding his head to no one in particular. "Storm's in the air. There's no mistaking."

He picked up his pace, as if to hurry the storm along, and his walk became erratic, almost frenetic, a kind of dance, and he stumbled on the uneven lawn, clutching at

Nash's coat sleeve for balance.

He looked up at his son with something like panic. "I get confused sometimes," he said. "Some days, I wake up thinking I'm a boy, and I can't wait to get outside to play. You know, my horse, grazing out by the barn."

"It's okay, Dad."

Alvin tightened his grip on Nash's jacket. "I just want to die here, in my own home."

A part of Nash wanted to tear away from his father's grasp, to run, and he hated himself for it.

Late into the afternoon came a knock at the door, and when Nash answered, he found Roy standing on the porch in uniform, his squad car parked out front.

"A farmer out by county line came across an abandoned pickup the other day. No plates. Called us to ask could he have it since it was left on his property."

Nash stared blankly at Roy.

The deputy waited him out for a bit, then continued. "Thought you might know something about it."

"Can't help you there."

"Ran a check on the serial number. Reason to believe it was involved in scam over in Indiana. An old lady hired some low-life outfit for home repair and got took. Pushed around, robbed."

"A truck was involved in all that?" Nash asked, shaking his head.

"There you go. Same old wiseass. Thought you might've mellowed a little. Should've know'd better."

"Listen, Roy. I had nothing to do with robbing some lady. That's a fact."

"Plenty in the department think different. They're looking to come down hard. Nash, if I was you, I'd kiss this town good-bye for keeps."

"Thanks for the warning," Nash said. "Seriously."

"It's just that we have a past, you and me, and, for what it's worth, I believe you, but I don't call the shots." Roy nodded to Nash, walked back to his patrol car, got in, and drove away.

Nash watched until Roy turned onto the main road then stood a while longer in the cold and thought about his options. He had done what he could to stop the road crew's thievery; he had no bad conscience in that regard. But the incident had convinced Nash to point the truck west toward Colorado, toward home, to make whatever peace he might.

When Nash went back inside the house, he found Alvin standing just inside the front door. "Trouble?" Alvin asked.

He seemed older somehow, and more frail. Nash wondered how much he had overheard.

"Nothing to worry about."

"Go on and take my truck, Son. God knows I got no

use for it. Why not just head on up the road a while."

Nash did not answer. He went into the kitchen and fixed Alvin an early dinner, a slab of ham and scrambled eggs with cheese, the simple fare they had lived on since being back together. Then he went to his room and packed his small duffel with the few clothes he owned and a small framed picture of Angelica and Robbie. When Nash returned to the kitchen, Alvin was sopping his plate with a piece of bread.

"Think I will take the truck. Got a few errands."

Alvin's eyes fell briefly to the duffel bag at Nash's feet. "It's gassed pretty near full," he said and, taking a bite of bread, turned his attention to the remnant of his meal.

Nash left Alvin at the table and walked out into the waning day. The temperature had dropped another ten degrees, to below freezing, he judged. He followed Highway 85 north out of the city. A light mix between sleet and snow began to fall as he drove toward Platteville. Three generations of Angelica's family still made their living in one manner or another from the land and in the small communities between Brighton and Greeley—farming, a little ranching, working in the tool-and-die shops, the gravel pits along the Platte River.

Nash followed 85 for several miles. A train passed him on the tracks paralleling the road to the east, and with the river turning course close by on the west, the cottonwoods growing tall along its banks, for a short stretch he felt hemmed in and claustrophobic. Past Fort Lupton, the land opened up again, and Nash pulled off the highway onto a country road that crossed the tracks heading east. The snow came a little heavier now, and the thickening clouds brought an early dusk. The falling light reminded him of that day three years ago. The weather had moved in fast. He had called Angelica and told her to go straight home from work; he would stop by Robbie's day care after his shift. Nash thought of the string of events that followed, how they just kind of stacked up, a series of minor errors in judgment. He had stopped after work for a quick beer because one of the boys had been promoted—one lousy beer, but enough to make him late—and the storm had strengthened in the short while he had been inside. It was a strange, malevolent storm. Ice coated everything—the trees, telephone lines, house eaves. And the damndest thing—he remembered seeing a bird tumbling from the sky as he hurried to pick up Robbie.

Slick roads, birds fluttering down with the snow—odd times.

The supervisor at day care was on edge when he arrived. "Six o'clock. We close at six. Not six-fifteen. And in this weather." She lectured him as if he were one of the children.

It aggravated the hell out of him. "Well, I won't be

taking any more of your time. You ready, boy? Let's get a move on."

He and Robbie walked hand in hand to the truck. Nash opened the door, and Robbie climbed into the front passenger seat. "Hold on there, cowboy. Your car seat is in the back."

But Robbie fussed. He had nearly outgrown the car seat and wanted no part of it. "Please? I want to watch the snow. I want to sit with you."

Just one beer. But if not for the beer, he would not have been in such a rush. He might not have relented when Robbie pleaded with him to sit up front. And if not for the time lost in the bar, he would not have driven so aggressively because he was irritated with the day care supervisor and because he was late and knew Angelica would be angry and worried. Nash remembered Robbie being excited about the snow.

"Can we make a snowman? Can we play?"

Nash had glanced over at his son just as he slid from his seat belt to the floor of the cabin to retrieve a pack of chewing gum—Nash had stuffed two pieces into his mouth to cover his beer breath before going into the day care and had tossed the pack onto the floor.

"In your seat, mister," Nash remembered scolding and reaching to yank his son up by the back of his jacket, then looking up as the deer came into the reach of his headlights and the instinctive jerking of the steering wheel and the uncontrollable gliding of the tires on the icy pavement.

He remembered coming to with the snow pelting his face. The cab of the pickup was open to the weather, and shards of glass lay scattered about the seat. He could not imagine what might have shattered the windshield, until his head cleared enough to look beside him for Robbie. He remembered screaming into the night, struggling with his seat belt, working his way from the wreckage, cutting his hands on the ragged edges of metal and glass, how his blood coagulated almost instantly in the cold. And no matter how hard he had struggled to forget, he remembered finding Robbie in the ditch and limping with him in his arms down the highway.

And afterward, the silent recriminations. No one directly blamed him for the accident. Accidents happen. Angelica tried to console him in spite of her own grief. Nash never mentioned his anger with the day care supervisor, how it fueled his recklessness. He never admitted his failure to secure Robbie into his car seat. He never confessed that the final words Robbie heard were a father's reproach. That knowledge he kept to himself, and the guilt ate away his insides like a cancer.

▶ ▶ ▶

Nash drove the country roads until he came to the small

cemetery that held the graves of Angelica's relatives. It was past dark, and the gate was locked. Nash parked the truck, cut the engine, and sat in silence for several minutes. Then he took a flashlight from the glove box, left the truck, and climbed the fence into the cemetery. He knew where the family plots were because he had, on occasion, accompanied Angelica when she paid respects to her grandparents, and it did not take him long to find Robbie's small marble headstone. A light shroud of snow covered the grave; just a hint of brown stubble poked through here and there.

Nash stood before his son's grave as the snow floated down. He thought about saying a prayer, seeking forgiveness, but he could find no words. What words were there when you've killed your child?

After a while, he dropped to his knees and placed his hand on the ground where he imagined his son's heart would be. His hand grew cold in the snow, but he did not raise it, could not raise it, and soon he imagined a warmth radiating up from the earth, up through his open palm, his arm, and into his own heart. He remained there, feeling connected to his son, while the snow continued to fall. When at last he rose to his feet, he saw that his palm print was traced clearly in the melted snow. He stood vigil before the grave into the night as the snow accumulated and slowly softened the print of a father's hand upon his son's heart.

Finally, Nash turned from the grave and retraced his steps back to the truck. After scraping ice from the windshield, he got in and cranked the engine. He worried briefly whether Alvin's ancient Ford would start in the cold, but his father had always taken care to maintain his vehicles, and it started without protest. Nash followed the route back to the highway. He paused at the intersection, flicking the turn signal first right, north, out of Colorado, then left, to Denver. He had done what he'd come to do; he had seen the people he needed to see. Every instinct told him to turn north, away from the trials that lay ahead if he remained—the law, his father's needs, Angelica's presence a constant pull on his heart. But after only a short deliberation, he turned back toward town, the town made so irredeemably a part of him by virtue of his son having lived and died there, and he drove on to finish what he had begun.

The Sea in These Hills

one

Just before daybreak, the cool of the night against his skin, Clayton stood on the dock watching fog rise off the marsh in phantom drifts. Then he stepped down into his johnboat and pulled the start cord on his outboard until it coughed to life, the guttural burble of the two-stroke engine disturbing the morning peace. He adjusted the fuel mix, unmoored, and guided his skiff along the tidal creek. The square bow pushed through tannin-stained water, creating a wake that slapped the banks. A muskrat slipped from its den and cut a vee in front of him. The fog and the dim light obscured landmarks, but Clayton had navigated these waters since he had turned seven years old. He knew every bend in the channel, every tree stump, every mudflat. Ten minutes from his dock, the creek opened

▶

into a shallow bay where storms regularly washed the ocean over the spit of land separating salt from freshwater, creating a brackish, life-rich estuary.

He looked out on that expanse of water and let his eyes scan the middle and far distances. Three miles across, flat and shallow—the deepest hole no more than twenty-two feet—six miles to the outlet that emptied into the bay. Swamp grasses and sedges grew on the banks, a barrier to civilization. On shore, the ancient seeping mud, gases swelling up from the decaying life; the shorebirds, feathery flashes moving through the reeds, wings catching the morning light. He imagined a teeming mix of fish, amphibians, crustaceans—a primeval, unknowable world below the brown surface. To the south, the water stretched to the horizon, the sound flowing into the bay, the bay into the ocean. To the west, a few pines rose from the far shores of the marsh where the wetlands began to recede, and to the east, on the spit of sand oceanside, shake-shingled summer cottages began to encroach upon the wild.

Nearing twenty-three, he had been away from the water only a few times: up to Richmond when his family had relocated after the war, two years in the army following high school, an apprenticeship at the Newport News shipyard. But duck season would come, and he would find himself in his reed-covered blind set on stilts in the middle of the sound while horizontal rain drove the birds toward his decoys. Early in the season came the fluttering, whistling teal, then later the gadwalls, the widgeons, and an occasional canvasback during the dark cold of winter. Or a summer run of bluefish would draw him back to surf-cast from the beach. Or his heart would yearn again for Loretta. Loretta. It was always one thing or another, but Loretta exerted the tidal pull.

He throttled the engine back at his first crab pot and grabbed the red cork buoy and drew up the line hand over hand until the wire mesh of his trap knocked against the gunwale. He unlatched the top flap of the pot and shook eight crabs out into a bushel basket. Then he pulled on his work gloves and reached down to cull the sooks from the jimmies, the females going into their own basket. The crabs scuttled and scratched against the slats of the crate, mandibles foaming, and they began latching onto one another with a clicking of claws. Clayton tossed back two undersized crabs then draped a water-soaked burlap bag over the crabs remaining in each basket. He rebaited the trap with a menhaden and eased it over the side. He worked down his line of crab pots, a dozen in this set, harvesting and sorting and baiting, then on to his next buoy line.

Clayton loved the sight of the blue crabs: the jimmies' green and white and light blue coloration, the sooks' brazen red claw tips. They were defiantly aggressive and presented an almost-prehistoric vision as they glided through the water on the fluttering paddles of their back swimming legs. Each crab represented a small but measurable contribution to his dream: for years, he had been squirreling away the quarters, the dollars, from selling his crabs, saving for a workboat that could carry him beyond the sound, into the Chesapeake. He knew the boat he wanted: a thirty-footer, mahogany-hulled with a cuddy, powered by a Cummings diesel, and equipped with a hydraulic line puller. It would allow him to set two hundred pots. A commercial crabbing license, a living. He had watched the *Misty Sue* put out from the docks for as long back as he could remember. It belonged to Hobby Eubank, who had worked the bay for fifty-five years but was so racked with arthritis that he could hardly keep his legs under him in a moderate chop. He looked to come in off the water. Clayton had talked to Hobby, and they had agreed on a price, and the old man said he would wait a bit so that Clayton could earn what he needed. A few years, at most. The sea was in the old man, after all, and wanting to give it up and actually doing it took a while to adjust to.

Off-season, Hobby let him work off some of the cost by helping him haul the boat to dry dock. They scraped barnacles and gave the hull a fresh coat of paint, a Carolina blue to the waterline, then white with gull-gray trim. They sanded down the work areas and revarnished them.

Here, on dry land, the feel of the decks against his cracked knuckles, the smoking engine he helped tune for another season on the water gave Clayton a sense of reality. He could envision himself in the cockpit, quartering into the swells. So the crabs were not just crabs to Clayton. They were his future.

By the time he finished his circuit, the fully risen sun had burned off the fog and almost three bushels of crabs quarreled in his baskets. Nine dollars, he reckoned, from Walter Pine and, if he was lucky, perhaps a few words, a veiled glance, from Loretta.

▶ ▶ ▶

Clayton tied his boat to the dock behind Walter's market and unloaded his crates. The day was early yet, before eight. He heard no stirring from the market, so he slipped a coin into the red machine on the porch and sat on the front step and drank his soda. Then he wet down his crabs from the outside spigot to keep them alive. A dead crab was worth nothing. The meat softened and spoiled so quickly that no one took a chance on cooking a dead crab. When Walter opened the shop, they would put the crabs in the ice room, where the cold slowed their metabolism and kept them alive for a day, maybe two.

Clayton soon heard sounds coming from inside, and Walter's voice—"I wish I could get them eggs done right just once"—and some scuffing of wood on wood. Clayton struck the front door with the flat of his hand, and after a minute, Walter appeared, red-faced and breathing hard.

"Got your crabs here."

Walter stood at the door in a white T-shirt stretched across his gut and dungarees held up with suspenders. One meaty arm rested on the side of the door frame, and a patch of belly escaped at his belt line. He paused, deciding whether to continue his business inside or to get on with the commerce of the day. Then his face loosened into a practiced smile, and he stepped down from the porch. "Well, hey there, young Clayton. Let's us take a look."

He bent over the basket and lifted the burlap bag covering the crabs. Clayton could see red scalp showing through his thinning white bristle. As Walter poked around the basket assessing the catch, Clayton looked past him to Loretta, who had come to the front door, barefoot, in a sleeveless shift. She crossed her arms at her chest and stared openly at Clayton. He noticed a welt rising on her right bicep and for a moment fought the urge to bring his elbow down into the small of Walter's back.

"I'll be straight with you, Son. Them's a right scrawny lot. I can go maybe eight dollars for the bunch."

They had been playing out this transaction for years, and they both knew within a narrow range what price they would settle on, but the game was expected, a part of doing business in southern Virginia in 1955.

"Yeah, you're probably right," Clayton said. "They are a little undersized. I should dump them all back into the bay to grow up."

"I might see my way to nine," Walter said, his voice taking on an edge. "Not a penny more. You going to drive me to the poorhouse, Son."

Clayton nodded, and Walter walked inside to retrieve the payment. Loretta stepped out of his way then came out onto the porch.

"Can you get free for a bit?" Clayton asked.

Loretta looked at him, sad-eyed, and suddenly a vacant ache lodged somewhere deep within him. Sun browned, pale eyed, strawberry-blond hair pulled into a simple ponytail with a strip of cloth, and freckles across the bridge of her nose, Loretta looked like a child. At twenty-one, she retained a girl's body, high cheeks, slim hips, small breasts unencumbered beneath her dress.

"I don't know. Maybe," she said. "He's talking about going over to Pungo to see about getting some sweet corn in for the weekend trade. I'll have to watch the store."

Clayton bent to retie his boot and caressed her calf as he stood, the soft, smooth curve of flesh that formed to his hand, a firm but giving warmth, sensual, promising. He backed away at the sound of Walter coming back from the cash register. He handed Clayton the money as a foreign sports car pulled into the parking lot and a man walked over to them. Clayton noticed the man's clothes: white bucks, white slacks, navy blazer.

"Hello, Walter."

"Good morning to you." Walter beamed at the man and spread his arms as if offering him all there was of the fine day. Gap-toothed, Walter had narrow-set eyes and a broad, unreadable face.

"Say, Walter, I'm having some people over to the cottage this evening. Do you have any crabs in?"

"Oh, yes, sir, Capt'n, I surely do." Walter made a great show of lifting the burlap from one of the baskets, and the man inspected the catch. "The boy here just brought them in. All number-one jimmies, biggest I seen this season. Ain't that right, Clayton?"

Clayton scuffed his shoe in the dirt and nodded.

"They'll do just fine. Can you bring them by this afternoon?"

"You bet, Capt'n." Walter turned to Clayton and clapped him on the shoulder, a bit too roughly for Clayton's liking. "Come on, Son, let's get these crabs into the icehouse."

▶ ▶ ▶

Midday, Clayton watched from a stand of pin oaks as Walter climbed into his truck and drove away, raising a plume of white dust from the crushed-shell roadbed. He emerged from the shadow of the trees into the glare of the day, the sun imposing a burdensome heat and the draining humidity dampening the neckline and underarms of his shirt by the time he reached the store.

Inside, Loretta sat on a stool behind the counter with a small rotating fan stirring her hair. As she tilted back her head to drink from a glass of lemonade, she noticed him. She lowered her glass to the counter and stood, and Clayton embraced her and tasted the tartness on her lips, her tongue, and he ran his hand down the smooth curve of her back and leaned to kiss the welt still showing on her arm.

She took his hand and pulled him toward the ice room. "Hurry. He won't be gone long."

two

Clayton had first laid eyes on Loretta five years earlier, in 1950. He and Sonny Ferrell were walking along the beach with their surf rods looking for a sign of feeding schools: oil slicks from bait fish that had been cut through by bluefish or kings, gulls diving on the cripples. Off to the south, toward the Carolina line, they tracked the black dot of a Ford pickup wending its way north, driving up the hard-packed sand at the tide line. The truck eventually pulled even with them, and a man older than Clayton's father, fifty or so, loose jowls, raised a finger to the bill of his cap. A black-and-tan coonhound occupied the passenger seat, its long face hanging from the window, ears flapping in the breeze. In the bed of the pickup, an aged lady and a young girl sat in rocking chairs, sharing space with two mattresses and a few wooden crates. Clayton's eyes were immediately drawn to the young girl, slender as a reed. She looked out to sea.

"Morning to you," the driver had said. Pointing to the surf rods, he asked, "Doing any good?"

"If you went by our luck," Sonny answered, "you'd swear there wasn't no fish in this pond at all."

"It goes that way some days, don't it? Say, boys, if I remember right, the cut to the road is around her somewhere, ain't it?"

"Yes, sir." Sonny pointed up the beach to where a boat was beached and two men were pulling in a seine hand over hand. A few townspeople were gathered to buy fresh fish. "Right across from them netters is the notch in the dunes. Blacktop picks up there into town."

"Obliged," the man said and tipped his hat again. "Be seeing you around."

He eased the truck into low gear, and as they pulled away, Clayton thought he noticed the young girl glance at him.

"What do you make of that?" he asked Sonny. Sonny was twelve years his senior, and Clayton often looked to him for advice.

"Just some more Tar Heels on their way to the land of plenty," Sonny answered.

"How old do you take her for?"

"The old lady?"

Clayton looked over at Sonny, dumbfounded.

Sonny smiled. "Fourteen, fifteen maybe. You best suck that tongue back inside your head before it gets all swol' up with sunburn."

They watched the truck leaving deep tracks in the sand, finally disappearing through a break in the dunes and onto the two-lane road that led to the small village of Sand Point, Virginia.

In town, Clayton learned that the man, Walter Pine, had purchased the old Henley market, a run-down store a mile inland, cinder block with a sheet-metal roof and living quarters in back. The store occupied a lot on the main drag into Sand Point but had remained vacant since old-man Henley passed, because people generally drove into the larger cities to do their grocery shopping. Walter decided to specialize and began selling fresh seafood to the natives and to the weekenders down from Norfolk and Virginia Beach. The store backed onto a channel that led to the bay, so he could buy local catches as well as those from trucking operations hauling from the Chesapeake. Eventually, he added crafts that appealed to the summer beach crowd: primitive watercolors, reed baskets, and hand-carved decoys Walter bought for pocket change from a one-eyed colored man who lived back in the swamp then sold to the tourists for a small fortune. Walter wore the veneer of southern geniality, so he was polite to strangers and was fawningly solicitous with customers. At the same time, he was vague with the townspeople about his motives for coming north. When neighbors stopped by with a covered dish or a dozen eggs to welcome the new family, Walter visited with them for a short time in the store or on the front stoop but never invited them back to their living quarters. Kept it general and polite and a bit at arms' length, by Virginia standards.

"We thank you for the cobbler. Blackberries do make a fine cobbler."

"Just a little something from me and the missus. Glad to see this store open again."

"We're happy to be here."

"Say, I had a cousin that married a Pine from down around Ocracoke Island. Name of Waverly, I believe, or Wesley. I ran into them a while back at a family picnic. I see some resemblance. You kin to him?"

"Not that I know of."

"He was thirty-five years with the Norfolk Southern line. Train people. He was missing a finger on each hand. Coupling the cars—let your mind wander one second and they get pinched right off when them cars come together."

"No, sir, I don't believe that would be my relations."

"Just the three of you then?"

"Just us."

"The elderly lady your mother?"

"Yes."

"And a fine daughter you got."

"Loretta Pine. Not a daughter. That would be my missus."

"Well, yes, of course."

▶ ▶ ▶

Clayton had been struck with Loretta from that first sight of her riding up the beach in the bed of the pickup. The way she sat in the rocker, the look in her eyes when she glanced his way suggested a noble suffering. He could not imagine how she had ended up as wife to an old man, and he was driven to meet her.

Shortly after Walter opened his market, Clayton came to ask about supplying him with crabs on a regular basis and also to again see this child bride that everyone was gossiping about. He had half expected that up close

Loretta would reveal herself old beyond her years, perhaps a little broad hipped and slow witted. Instead, he found a girl whose pure looks and mature bearing struck him dumb.

She was ladling ice chips into the seafood display when he entered. "Need something?" she asked, glancing up from her work.

"Come to see Mr. Pine. Business." Clayton was tall for seventeen, with a lanky, athletic frame. But when the girl looked at him, he suddenly felt awkward.

"Mr. Pine is out back, seeing to the dock."

She returned to her ladling, and Clayton watched her, the smooth curve of her back, her forearms flexing with her efforts. He stood silent for a minute or two, glancing now and again out the single window in the small store, down at his feet, trying not to stare, but his eyes would turn back to her. He could not help himself.

"You could walk out back to see him."

"Pardon?"

"Mr. Pine. Out back, by the dock."

"Oh," Clayton said and turned for the door and went around the building to where he found Walter hollering orders to two skinny boys standing waist deep in the water, sinking pilings into the mud with a sledgehammer. Their brown backs shone with sweat. A blue heron waded on the far bank stalking frogs and small fish in the shallows.

"Line up them pilings true," Walter called to the boys from the shade of a wild plum tree where he sat in a metal lawn chair. "Sink 'em deep. I don't want it floating away with the first blow."

Clayton stood off to the side and waited as Walter mopped his face with a rag, swabbed his fleshy neck, and rested a hand on the shelf of his gut, which was round and taut as a watermelon. He appraised Clayton.

"Do I know you, boy? You look familiar."

"No, sir. I mean, we talked a bit on the beach the other day. I'm Clayton Royster from over around Nemo."

"I heard of the name. Your daddy farm?"

The simple mention of his father's name caused Clayton to pause, and a part of him went back to better times, lean but happy, when there was the land and the water at the far end of the property. At the thought, he experienced something like homesickness. "Used to, part-time. Beans and corn, mostly. Took us up to Richmond after the war for a state government job. I came back."

"Where you staying?"

"Around. Mostly at Sonny Ferrell's. I work over at his Esso station after school. He keeps a room for me." Clayton stopped then, uncertain how to continue. They watched the boys in the water, one holding the piling steady, the other pounding with the sledge, the sharp report of hammer against wood like claps of thunder.

"You want to be a farmer too?" Walter asked, looking back at Clayton.

"No, sir. I'm a waterman. Sonny says I was born to it. I was thinking you could use some crabs now and then. For the store."

They lapsed again into silence while Walter considered the proposition. He rolled over onto one haunch and stuffed the rag into his back pocket. "Maybe, if the price is right. In season, for the weekend trade."

"I'll come by with a mess on Friday."

"Mostly jimmies I'm interested in. Bring them on over, I'll see what you have. No promises."

Walter turned his attention to the boys, signaling the end to their transactions. Clayton went back around front and fought the urge to reenter the store, but when he walked past the window, he caught Loretta looking out at him.

Friday, when he brought his blue crabs to the market, Walter met him on the front stoop and settled up with him right there. Clayton kept looking around the bulk of him, attempting to catch sight of Loretta.

"Maybe I'll use some of this money here to buy a flounder filet for supper."

"Fresh out of flounder."

"Croaker?"

"Nope." Walter continued to block the entrance. "I

might could use another bushel of crabs tomorrow."

"I'll bring them by."

The next day, again no Loretta. Nor the next. Friday, Saturday, Sunday deliveries through June and into July, no Loretta. Always Walter or his mother minding the store. And with every missed visit, Clayton grew more desperate to see her, unsure just why, but desperate nonetheless.

Finally, one Saturday afternoon midmonth, he happened to notice Walter at the service station in Pungo, his truck up on jacks and a mechanic's feet sticking out from the undercarriage. Walter and Sonny were standing by the pump with bottles of cola. Walter's mother sat in the shade of the roof overhang looking dour. Clayton drove straightaway to Walter's seafood market. Loretta was minding the counter, tending to a customer, wrapping a whole bluefish in newspaper. When the customer left, Loretta looked at Clayton. Her expression revealed a neutral recognition.

"Hey," he said.

"Hey. Mr. Pine's not around just now."

"Oh, that's all right, nothing important to see him about."

Clayton milled about the small store, fingering a carved-wood decoy, examining the contents of the ice case: a few flounder arranged like cards fanned out on a table, three bug-eyed striped bass looking out at him, a handful of softshell crabs Clayton himself had brought in early that morning, and a bucket of oysters.

"You need anything from there?" she asked.

Clayton straightened and looked at her. She looked back. She seemed in no rush to have him gone or to get back to her chores.

"I haven't seen you around lately," he said.

"I've been right here."

"Just not when I'm bringing crabs to Mr. Pine."

"I've seen you. From the back room."

"You didn't come out to say hello."

"No."

She brushed back a strand of hair that had fallen across her forehead, then came from around the display case and leaned back against the front counter. Clayton held his breath at the grace of her simple movement.

"Mr. Pine generally wants me in the back when men are about."

"I don't expect he'll want you in school this fall neither, will he?" Clayton was a rising senior and figured Loretta to be a year or two behind him.

"No."

"Is that all right by you?"

"Doesn't matter. I'm his wife."

"Still."

Clayton wanted to continue, would have stood all

afternoon making small talk, any excuse to keep her standing in front of him. And she seemed willing to let him. But the sound of a vehicle pulling up in front of the store interrupted them. For an instant, Clayton saw fear cross Loretta's face, and she hurried to the window.

"A customer. That's all." Her shoulders relaxed.

"I best be on my way."

Clayton crossed to the door, but before he left, she said something to him that caused him to question his own hearing, to play it over again and again in his mind that day and on through a restless night.

"Mr. Pine is taking his momma to the doctor's Monday afternoon up in Norfolk. She's been feeling poorly. I'll be tending the market."

▶ ▶ ▶

They took to meeting in the ice room. Just to talk at first. It was cool but not cold, with a small window giving view of the parking lot and a back door kept bolted from the inside. If a customer drove up, or if it was nearing time for Walter's return, Clayton could slip out the back and Loretta could return to the store with a bucket of ice chips for the seafood display case. The room contained a small table used to sort crabs, dress fish, shuck oysters. When Clayton visited, she covered the table with a red-checkered oilcloth. She would open the soda dispenser with her restocking key and take out two soft drinks, and they would sit and talk softly at the table as might a couple at an outdoor café. Loretta would quiz Clayton about school and life on the water. Especially the water.

"My daddy took me out with him fishing once," she told him.

"Once?"

"Just the once. When I was five. Said that was the first and last of it."

"Why?"

"Said I scared him to death. I didn't have enough fear of the sea. Whenever he throttled back to check a net, I kept trying to climb down the stern ladder into the water. I remember." Loretta was looking out the window of the icehouse, eyes distant, reaching into memory. "Offshore, the sea was so blue and clean. I wanted to dangle my feet in it. It looked almost solid enough to walk on."

"I'll take you out sometime."

"I'd like that more than anything. But I don't know."

▸ ▸ ▸

They met once or twice a week through the waning of summer. It was not often that both Walter and his mother were away. As the old woman became more infirm, Clayton occasionally chanced a visit when he knew she would be resting, but those times Loretta always acted more reserved and wary, ducking frequently from the ice room to check on her mother-in-law. On these visits, Loretta reminded him of a small bird, nervous and darting, and he felt guilty for putting her at risk.

When they had time, Clayton pressed Loretta about her life. He would ask her anything at all to listen to her voice, full of drawn-out vowels and soft consonants.

Over time, he pieced together her story. Her father, a commercial fisherman out of Oregon Inlet, had gone over the side during a gale. His mate hauled him from the sea and revived him, but he was left feebleminded and invalid. When Walter approached her father about the offer of marriage to Loretta with a monthly stipend attached, he seemed befuddled by the question and mumbled something about Loretta taking in his laundry. But Loretta grasped the intent and recognized a solution for two problems at once: one less mouth to feed at home and a steady, if meager, flow of cash. Although Loretta had been her father's favorite, he was beyond the ability to protest, and her mother had four younger children to think about.

Loretta had run away from Walter when he first imposed himself on her (Clayton was unsure what this meant, and Loretta had to explain to him, "He had his way with me as a husband's right with his wife," and Clayton had flinched at the image of Walter rutting and sweating atop her), and again after the first time he had disciplined her (for being smart-mouthed). Her mother had taken her back without reproach, but after a few months of doing without Walter's stipends, Loretta returned to him, contrite and submissive, for the good of the family. She explained herself to Clayton, evenly, without emotion, so he would understand exactly where she stood.

"Last time I went back to Mr. Pine, I promised my daddy I'd see it through until the young ones were of working age."

"He agreed?" Clayton asked.

"He couldn't understand all of what I was saying."

"Your mother?"

"I never asked what she thought. I wouldn't put her to the test like that. But it's an oath just the same. A promise. Blood to blood. I won't break it. I'll not forsake my kin. Not for anything."

Clayton marveled at Loretta's allegiance. His own parents had had need of him also. His father, a soft-spoken, amiable farmer, had returned from the war withdrawn and sullen. He had lost thirty pounds overseas and was unable to regain it. Periodically, he would rally his strength, then fade, becoming so weak and palsied at times that he could not work the farm at all. He would sit in the front room of the farmhouse in his "Sunday" chair and stare down at his shaking hands and talk under his breath, as if trying to lecture himself to health. The neighbors pitched in when they could during the sowing and harvesting, but the farm took on a neglected look. Fencing went unmended, thistle and creeping vine overtook fallow sections. They hung on for a few years, and as Clayton grew older, he worked the fields tirelessly. But following an especially bad soybean harvest in the fall of 1949, his father sold out and moved the family to Richmond so he could take a desk job with the state agriculture department near the veteran's hospital.

Without the fields to work and the waters to ply, Clayton found his new home a somber and lifeless place. He took refuge in a wood that bordered his neighborhood. Walking among the pine mixed with sweet gum and the occasional stand of maple, he hunted snakes and camped on weekends even as the weather turned. One time, deep in the woods on a hummock that could have been a Civil War battlement, he found an old tin cup and three musket balls fused by rust. He kept to himself and stayed away from home; he found the sight of his withering father almost unbearable.

One day, he returned from school to find his father cleaning a service revolver on the kitchen table. He never knew his father owned a revolver. The disassembled cylinder sat upright beside an oilcan, and the empty chambers looked menacing.

"Dad, what are you doing?"

"It's important to keep your weapon clean. The mud and dirt could jam it. Cost you your life."

More and more frequently, his father would retreat into the bedroom after dinner. Clayton and his mother would listen from behind the closed door to the metallic clicks of the revolver being broken down and reassembled.

"I can hardly stand this," Clayton told his mother one day. "I have to go home."

"This is your home."

"You know what I mean."

"You can't leave," his mother said. "He's better when you're around. You bring him joy. Can't you see it?" Clayton's mother beamed at him and nodded her head frantically. As Clayton's father had grown more withdrawn and silent, his mother had become buoyant with nervous optimism.

"That's not true. Don't say that. I have to get out of here. It's not my responsibility."

"Of course it is, honey. It is your duty. You're daddy's boy. His joy."

Clayton lasted there a year but could neither accept his role in Richmond nor purge the ocean from his blood.

The day after he turned fifteen, he left a note and hitchhiked back to Sand Point, and Sonny took him in. He wrote home, Sonny insisted on it, visited on holidays, and telephoned once a month as expenses allowed. But the clipped conversations over the static lines shamed more than comforted him, especially on his father's bad days.

During his visits with Loretta, Clayton found himself unable to talk to her about his family. After what she had sacrificed, he felt unworthy.

▸ ▸ ▸

Autumn signaled the end of the tourist season, the end of Walter's need for crabs, the end of Clayton's excuse for coming around the market. Summer cottages were boarded up for the winter against the northeasters that roared down the bay. The stream of cars from inland eased to a trickle.

"Come see me next May," Walter told Clayton the second week in September.

As usual, Loretta was nowhere in sight.

"Thought you might need some help around the store in the off-season. Painting, roof work?"

"No. Guess I can get by on my own. Just come by next summer."

And so the winter came, damp and chilly, a dull gray for days on end. Virginia winter: neither the mild, subtly disturbing inconveniences of the South nor the deep, numbing cold of the North, but a humid, seeping chill and a nagging discomfort punctuated by fierce storms that turned beach sand into a honeycomb of ice from the frozen spray blowing in off the sea.

Months crept by. Clayton passed his eighteenth birthday and added an inch and ten pounds to his frame. No visits with Loretta and only a few glimpses of her during that cold time—a quick glance when they stopped for gas at Sonny's and Clayton happened to be pumping; they passed in the grocery aisle once in February, but Walter was leading Loretta and she did not even acknowledge Clayton when Walter nodded to him, and Clayton fretted that she may have forgotten him altogether.

He helped at the Esso station after school and stayed with Sonny and his wife, a kind-spirited, quiet woman with an open, plain face made pretty by her disposition. He slept in the spare bedroom that they planned for a child that had not yet come.

Clayton could hear them talking at night. They were young still, they told themselves while sitting on the front porch in metal garden chairs sipping sweet tea during the reassuring warmth of early summer. Just thirty. Time enough. And when the crickets started up at dusk and the frogs from the marsh kicked in and the lightning bugs blinked on and off like stars come to visit, they believed what they told themselves. But during the dark season, the quickening night, without the comfort of the porch and the warmth of the sun, they both secretly doubted, and they liked having Clayton around.

Sonny treated Clayton like a younger brother, and Clayton respected him and tried to stay even keeled, but Sonny took note of Clayton's moodiness as winter deepened.

"You been sulking around like you lost your favorite hunting dog."

"It's just the weather. I get down when I can't be out and about."

"Wouldn't have anything to do with that girl over to the market?"

"Who?"

"Never mind. It's just that nothing good ever comes from mooning after something that can't be yours."

"I swear, Sonny, sometimes I don't have no idea in hell what you're talking about."

▶ ▶ ▶

In April, word came that Walter's mother had died, and the store was left vacant for a month while Walter and Loretta carted her back to North Carolina to plant her in home soil. Some speculated that the Pines might not return.

The thought of not seeing Loretta again affected Clayton strangely. At first, her absence felt like a great weight in his limbs. Walking was a labor, like wading waist deep against a riptide. Simple tasks, repairing a damaged crab trap, seemed exhausting beyond comprehension.

But soon, surprisingly soon, the burden lifted and he felt lighter, as if he had shed pounds and pounds. His spirits also lifted. He noticed a girl in his class at school. Instead of lurking in the scrub behind the store hoping to catch sight of Loretta hanging wash or dumping trash, he began to spend time on the water again, appreciating the bloom of the wild azaleas along the banks and the honeysuckle veining boathouses and dock posts.

Then, in late May, the pickup appeared back at the store and Clayton was overcome with the old single-minded urge.

On Memorial Day weekend, cars repopulated the winding road to Sand Point and cottages were reopened, aired out. Clayton resumed his crabbing. It was a busy time for Walter, taking orders and, when requested, making deliveries to the cottages. On Saturday, after watching Walter pull out of the lot with several crates of seafood in the bed of his truck, Clayton approached the storefront warily, unsure how he would be received. Would she remember him at all? Still wish to talk? He entered quietly. No one was minding the counter.

"Hello?" he called, his voice sounding to him high and squawking.

Loretta came out from the back rooms. Her hair was down and longer than last September, and her body had filled out so that she looked more woman now than girl.

"Hey there," he said.

Loretta walked over to him and kissed him hungrily. "Tell me," she demanded, "I need to know right now. Do you have a girl?"

"I don't have one. Not a one."

"Did you like what I just did?"

"I did."

"Do you want me to do it again?"

Clayton gave her question serious consideration. He had dreamt of her almost every night since he had first seen her, often awoke in the hours before dawn in an agitated and aroused state. Spotted sheets some mornings, damp evidence of his obsession. A part of him wanted her more than he could ever explain. Another part of him thought this was wrong, no matter what his desires. He sensed that the answer to her question might set the course for the rest of his life.

"I do. Yes. Thank you."

▸ ▸ ▸

In June, Clayton graduated from high school, and by summer's end, his draft notice arrived in the mail. He and Loretta began taking chances they never would have before. Clayton slipped into the market when Walter ran errands, knowing he could return at any minute. A few rushed embraces, fumbling hands over sheathed breasts, kisses, then out and away before they were caught. Once they even met while Walter was drunk and passed out in the back room, his snoring an ironic sentry to their hurried union.

Just before he left for basic training, with Walter gone in to Virginia Beach to see about extending a loan, Loretta led Clayton to the ice room and guided him into territory they had not traveled before. Walter would be gone for hours; they had time. Loretta drew her shift up over her head and let it drop to the floor.

Her experience surprised Clayton, secrets that were only talked about in whispers among the boys. Then it came to him: she was a married woman. She knows. She led his hands to her body and told Clayton where to go and what to do.

"Slower now. Here. Now here. That's right."

When they had finished, she murmured into his neck. "I had to be the first for you. That way, you'll always remember me."

"I'll always remember you anyway. You have to know that."

▶ ▶ ▶

Army service passed in a slow blur for Clayton: basic training and a time spent in the supply pool at Fort Eustis. He could not write Loretta, could not even chance calling her. She sent the occasional letter, but even then not from the local post office—word would get around. Not being able to answer ate at him. On the occasional furlough, he would stop by the market on the pretense of talking shop with Walter, reminding him that his tour would be up before they knew it, and he hoped Walter would have need of his crabs when he returned. He rarely even caught a glimpse of Loretta.

The threat of deployment to Korea hung over the whole of his tour. One day rumors would fly through camp that a treaty had been signed only to be replaced the next with a solemn confirmation that they would be shipped out the first of the month. The teenager in Clayton hungered for the test of battle; the man in him had nightmares about the horrifying accounts he had read of places with melancholy and foreboding names: Heartbreak Ridge, Bloody Ridge.

In October of 1952, rumor spread around camp that orders were coming down the line any day now. On a three-day pass, Clayton took a bus to Richmond and visited his parents. He needed his father, his advice. He had been to war, and Clayton was now very frightened.

When he walked into the kitchen, his mother looked up from her cooking as if he were just home from school. Vacantly, distractedly, she said, "Oh, hi there, you."

Clayton walked over to her and gave her a kiss on the

top of her head. "Where's Dad?"

"Oh, he's been busy. Able to work most days now. Should be home in a bit."

Clayton poured tea from the fridge into a glass, added a lemon wedge, and sat on the front porch, waiting. A half hour later, he saw a man walking up the road from the main-street bus station. The man wore a gray flannel suit, baggy, too large for his frame, and a fedora pulled low over his face. Stooped, he leaned into his gait as if fighting a strong wind. The old man turned into his parents' front walk and eased his way up the porch steps.

"Dad?"

"Why, hello, Clayton. Look at you. The uniform."

"Remember, I called you. The draft."

"Yes, of course."

"I might just be shipping out in a short while."

"European theater?"

"Korea."

"Oh, yes."

His father looked into Clayton's eyes, searching for something, Clayton thought, then turned away and stared out over the porch railing, unfocused.

"What's it like?"

His father stayed silent for a long while. Clayton thought maybe he had not heard his question.

"You'll get by."

"But how?"

"Any way you know. Anything it takes. You just do it."

Clayton returned to camp, but the orders never came. Just day after day in the supply pool, loading pallets of rations and blankets to be shipped overseas. Day after day of routine boredom punctuated now and again with the rumors of deployment.

And always, the dreams of Loretta, the feel of her body, the arch of her back as she reached her hips for him. He tried to use his army time to wean himself from a sea that he realized held little promise of a livelihood these days. But the lure was too great. Finally, he was discharged, and Clayton returned to Sand Point and to the water he loved and the girl he could not give up.

three

Now, two years out of the army and they were still meeting in the ice room, Clayton twenty-three and anxious, his life seemed to be spinning in circles, wanting Loretta. The early days of groping and fumbling had been replaced by a practiced efficiency. However, the opportunity for meeting was limited by Walter's increasing possessiveness of Loretta as he grew older and she bloomed into adulthood. She remained resigned to the oath she made her father.

"Let's leave this place?" Clayton asked her again after they had done what they had come into the ice room to do. Her dampness clung to him. Their smells intermixed. He could not distinguish himself from her.

He thought of Hobby's workboat. He could probably borrow the balance he needed from Sonny. With a boat and his crab pots, he could make a living up and down the coast.

"I can be happy away from here if you are with me," he said. "We'll go down to Carolina. I can put the boat out of Oregon Inlet. Or up bay, out of Crisfield. … I could be happy anywhere," he repeated.

"Be happy here, now, with what we have."

"I try, but I want more."

A sound from the front of the store startled them both. Loretta grabbed a bucket of ice chips and Clayton ducked from sight as she threw open the door. Walter leaned against the counter. His face was beet red; sweat dripped from his nose onto the counter, the huge barrel of his midsection heaving like a bellows.

"Mr. Pine, I thought you were headed to Pungo."

"Goddamned truck quit on me two miles out. Had to walk back. In this goddamned heat. Zed Phelps passed me right by and did not stop. I'll remember that son of a bitch."

"Let me get you a cool drink."

"Bring me a beer."

"I don't think there's any beer."

"There's beer. I know I left some. You been drinking my beer?"

"You know I haven't."

"The hell I do. Now find me a beer."

"I can't find what's not there."

"Watch that smart mouth of yours." Walter stomped into the living quarters, and the sounds of his rummaging followed him through the rooms. A glass crashed to the floor. "Goddamn!"

He returned and gripped Loretta's bicep. "Where's my beer?!"

The bucket she held slipped from her grasp, sending ice chips skating across the wooden floor.

"There you go," said Walter and clapped her on the ear with the flat of his hand.

He hit her again, and the administration of punishment seemed to invigorate him. He grunted like a hog and rose up on his toes to strike her again, but Clayton came up behind him and swung a wooden duck decoy at the back of his head with such force the duck's head snapped from its body. Walter's hulk seemed to topple in slow motion, wavering slightly, then sort of folding in on itself like an imploded building. On the way down, his head struck the corner of the countertop, opening a gash in his scalp. Blood began pooling on the rough planks as soon as his body settled to the floor. Clayton stood over him, still holding the splintered decoy and sucking for air.

Loretta bent over Walter. "Lord Jesus, what have you done?"

"He was hitting on you."

"It was nothing."

"Is he dead?"

"Oh, Lord, you shouldn't have hit him."

"I couldn't help it."

"Go. You have to go."

"What if he comes around?"

"It'll be worse if you're here. Go."

"What if he's dead?"

"I don't know. Lord, what am I going to do? Clayton, go."

"Come with me."

"Go."

Clayton allowed her to push him from the room, and once outside, he ran. He made his way to Sonny's garage and found him in the small office at the metal desk thumbing through receipts.

"Hey, boy. You're all red in the face. You been running around in this heat?"

Clayton was unsure why he had come to Sonny or what he intended to say to him, but he felt ready to explode, and he blurted out, "Sonny, I think I might've just killed a man!"

Sonny put down his pencil and stood from his desk. "Walter Pine?"

"What makes you say that?"

Sonny just shook his head and said, "You got a lot to learn, Son."

"He beat her, Sonny."

"She's his wife."

"I don't even remember what happened, exactly."

Clayton's legs were moving in place, as if his muscles were still twitching to run, and he looked off in the direction of the salt marsh.

Sonny walked around the desk to face him straight on. "I best drive over to the market and see what's going on. You stay out on the water until after dark. Come in the back door."

Sonny left, and Clayton took the small pram he kept in a side channel behind Sonny's garage out into the marsh. He sat at the square bow and sculled the boat silently forward holding a single short-handled paddle in one hand and carving S-shapes through the water. He stayed in the narrow cuts where larger motor-powered crafts could not navigate.

The still air held the odor of decay—rotting vegetation, marsh gases seeping up through the mud. It made him think of death. But out here, death seemed so natural, so much a part of the landscape, it calmed him. A shore-bird hatches its eggs in the reeds; a chick squawks and is fed masticated snail and worm, and after a few weeks, it tests its growing strength by flopping from the nest onto the mud; a heron that had been standing stone still in the shallows waiting for prey spears the chick with one lightning stab of its beak and carries it back to its nest to feed its own chicks.

He spent the afternoon numbly recounting what he might have done otherwise back there. Should he have called out to Walter? Grabbed his arm? And Loretta, what of her? She seemed upset that Clayton had struck Walter. He wished he had stayed at the market to sort out their troubles, to decide together what to do.

The day waned. A hazy sun dipped beneath the line of loblolly pines on the western horizon, and as dusk settled, Clayton watched a raccoon at the bank of the creek pin a fiddler crab to the mud and expertly dissect it. A red-winged blackbird perched on a cattail, a vague presence in the dimming light except for the red patch that reminded Clayton of blood and prompted him to turn the pram back toward Sonny's garage.

Sonny was at the kitchen table when Clayton entered. He pointed Clayton to a chair and handed him a beer and took one himself.

"Well," Sonny said, "I guess the good news is, you didn't kill the man."

Clayton's hands began to shake so violently that the beer can rattled on the table. Both men drank and then stared down at the table.

"Thank God. I would not have wanted that on my mind. How bad off is he?"

"Conscious. Bandaged up. Doc said maybe a concussion. He wouldn't go to the hospital."

Sonny drank again and retrieved another beer and looked to Clayton, who motioned no.

"Sheriff was there. Came when they called the ambulance. Don't know what Walter told him, but he didn't ask me your whereabouts. Damndest thing, though. After the sheriff left, Walter told me he knew what had happened. He said that you had better go see him in the morning. You two had something to settle."

"Well, then. That's good."

"I'll be going with you."

"No, Sonny. It's been like we've been in this kind of dance for a while now. I guess it's time to see how it plays out."

The night never cooled, and Clayton lay sweating in his bed in Sonny's spare room listening to the frogs and the crickets, sleeping in fits, dreaming he could somehow communicate with Loretta using his own night sounds to comfort and reassure her. At four, he rose and dressed and slipped out of Sonny's house. He took his boat and navigated the night out into the bay and around the shoreline to the canal that led to Walter's dock and then rested until full light.

Walter was waiting at the open door of the market when Clayton came around from the dock. His head was wrapped in clean white gauze and the side of his face was slightly swollen, but his eyes appeared clear and sharp. Walter looked down at Clayton and smiled as if he were greeting a loyal customer.

"Looks like another hot one, don't it, Son?"

Clayton remained silent and came to the door.

"Come on in, and let's have us a talk. You gave me a pretty good thump yesterday."

"You shouldn't hit her."

They went into the market, and Walter locked the door and hung the Closed sign in the window then went and stood beside a small display table that had been cleared of goods. He leaned both hands on the table and bent toward Clayton, and his voice took on a pedantic tone, as if he were explaining something to an uncomprehending child. "Loretta is a nice girl, but she is headstrong at times. She needs to be righted. She's a baby yet, still learning how to be a good wife."

Walter's voice was even and conversational, and his

face displayed no sign of anger. "Sometimes she gets tempted to sin. You're older. You should know better than to covet something that ain't yours."

Clayton felt a growing discomfort at the seeming depth of Walter's knowledge about him and Loretta, and then suddenly stupid for ever thinking a secret could be kept in a town like Sand Point, where everyone knew everyone else and it took only one person noticing an indiscretion for the entire town to soon learn of it.

"What do you want of me?" Clayton asked.

"Me and the sheriff had a nice talk yesterday. A good boy, the sheriff. Told him I'd take care of my own business, and if I needed him, I'd let him know. He was okay by that."

"What do you want?" Clayton repeated.

Walter rose from the table and turned to the back room. He still wore that affable expression, though his voice deepened when he called out, "Loretta, come on out here!"

Loretta walked slowly from the living quarters, each step measured and careful. Clayton looked to her for a sign, some indication of what she expected of him. Her face was blank. She came up and stood beside Walter and looked off over Clayton's shoulder.

"Loretta, honey, you my wife, ain't you?"

"I am, Walter."

"You want to keep it that way?"

"Yes."

"You know it's my duty as husband to lead you, to show you right from wrong?"

"Yes, Walter."

"Discipline?"

"Yes."

"Go get the strap."

Loretta went behind the counter beside the cash register and brought out a worn-leather razor strop, three inches wide, two feet long, and handed it to Walter. He took the strap and nodded to the table. Loretta bent over the table and lifted her shift above her hips, braced herself on her elbows, and offered herself up to Walter. She wore no underwear.

"Son of a bitch, I will kill you!" Clayton said, and started toward Walter.

Loretta jerked her face up and glared at him, and her expression riveted Clayton in place. A fierce challenge, a mix of humiliation and determination. Hate. For him? Walter? Both? And a warning: *Don't you dare. Don't you dare move. Don't you dare come between my kin and me. Don't you dare break my blood oath.* But something more, something that haunted Clayton whenever he thought back on this day. *This is my future,* she seemed to say through her eyes. *I am somebody here. A shop owner's wife, and I will not trade it for you.*

Clayton stood there watching as Walter caressed the smooth white flesh of Loretta's buttocks as if he were stroking his hound. Walter looked down at her offering, the smile still pasted but the eyes hardening, seeming almost inquisitive, evaluating what was before him. Then he stepped back, lifted the strap, and brought it down across Loretta's haunches. Clayton jumped with pain, but Loretta did not change expression. She kept her eyes on Clayton's eyes, and the strap came down again. Her jaw struck forward a bit, but she did not flinch; she continued to hold Clayton in place with her eyes. Walter administered one more lash and then came up close behind Loretta so that his crotch obscenely nudged her raised backside, and he rested his hand gently on Loretta's waist.

He looked at Clayton. "Tell you what, boy. You still around town tomorrow, come on by and we'll continue our discussion. Still around the day after, more of the same. You understand me, boy?" Walter's smile was gone now.

Clayton tried to avert his eyes from Loretta, his shame was so great, but she would not allow it, would not offer him the comfort of lowering her gaze. The pain in his soul grew, fed from the pain in her eyes, and the resignation. He backed out of the market, and once outside, stumbled to his boat, vomited into the water, and made his way back to Sonny's. He gathered his clothes in his duffel and left the house and began running again, and this time he did not stop.

▶ ▶ ▶

Clayton hitchhiked into Norfolk and worked briefly at day labor for a moving-van company and then in a warehouse across from the freight docks, sleeping in doorways and in the Greyhound lobby until he scraped together enough to buy a rusted-out old Plymouth sedan from someone who seemed more down and out even than he. He had left Sonny's with his life's savings, the savings for the work-boat. Together with his earnings, he had traded his dream for a broken-down heap. He realized he needed to escape the sea. Everything about it—the smell of salt in the air, the shriek of gulls, the watermarks on the wharf rising and receding with the tides, the same lunar pull he felt working in his own blood—tormented him with reminders of a life now irrevocably changed. He knew that if he stayed in Norfolk for long, the sea would eventually lure him back to Sand Point, back to Loretta; he could hear its call in his sleep. But the trade seemed cruel and unfair.

He pointed the car west and drove with only a vague notion of destination. When he pulled into the driveway in Richmond and turned off the ignition, he was genuinely surprised to find himself in front of his parents' house.

He sat for a few minutes in the car, gaining his bearings, listening to the motor shudder to a stop. It was midafternoon, the heat slanting in from the west. The front lawn was overgrown and brown-yellow, unhealthy. The house was quiet when he entered through the front screen door. There were no domestic sounds or smells. He called to his mother and his father. No answer. The living room was tidy but sterile. Nothing out of place, but no feel of life—no magazines on the tables, no books, no everyday clutter, no smell of tobacco or aftershave or furniture oil. Just a vague antiseptic odor, like rubbing alcohol or camphor lotion. He walked through the kitchen and found his mother sitting on the back porch shelling peas into a colander she held in her lap.

"Hi, Mom. Don't get up."

"Dear, what a surprise." His mother's hand darted to her cheek then out to touch his arm. "Why didn't you call, give me a chance to tidy up your room, clean sheets, cook a real meal? We're just having meatloaf, these peas, some mashed potatoes. You'd of called, I would have made that roast you like so much. Why, let's look at you."

Clayton leaned down to embrace her then sat beside the chair and took a handful of peas from a brown grocery bag and began popping the skins and scraping the pods into the colander with his thumb. "Haven't had a chance to call in a few weeks. How's things?" he asked.

"Fine, real fine," she answered. "Your dad, he's doing great. Almost back to his old self, in my thinking. Appetite like a farmhand. Are you hungry? There's leftovers in the fridge. Sweet tea? Could you eat a bite?"

"He at work?"

"Well, no. I don't believe he went in today."

"Upstairs resting?"

"I think he's out for a stroll. He's taken to walking lately. Like I told you, almost back to his old self. Always up and going, it seems. Won't hardly sit still."

"Where?"

His mother looked at him, confused.

"Dad, where he go walking?"

"Out back in the woods. I saw him take that path leading south. Not sure where he wanders from there, but sometimes he's gone for a long spell. I think the exercise must be good for him, don't you? Perks you up, takes your mind off problems, don't you think?"

"Sure, Mom."

Clayton stood and went back into the house and took a long drink from the kitchen faucet, bending to the stream of water, letting the cold wash over his face. He wandered through the rooms, trying to absorb a sense of place, recognize a familiar sight or feel, a picture on the wall, anything to tie it to home. On his father's smoking table beside his recliner, Clayton noticed a tin button, old and battered, with ornate scrolling etched into it, and he remembered finding something like that long ago. He knew where to find his father.

He went back out to the porch and put a hand on his mother's shoulder. "Think I'll have a look," he said.

He walked across the backyard and through a strip of field grass and into the woods. In the shade of the trees, the heat lifted. The trail, carpeted with pine needles and matted leaves from seasons past, finally connected him to this place. The tension he did not even realize he carried began easing from his shoulders and back.

He came upon his father where he knew he would: on the earthen embankment Clayton had discovered when they had first moved up here. His father seemed not so much older as emptier than when last he had visited, like something had been drained from him so that he seemed to slump inward, disappearing into himself, shrunken.

"Dad."

His father looked up at him and his eyes did brighten. "Son. Come sit. Good to see you."

"You've discovered my secret place. Remember? I showed you the tin cup and the musket balls I found here."

His father did not answer, and Clayton could not tell if he remembered or not.

Then his father looked off into the distance and

began rocking in place. "Men died here," his father said. "And boys."

"How do you know that?"

"I can feel them under my feet. Not six feet down. This is hallowed ground."

His father continued the slow rocking that reminded Clayton of silent mourners at a funeral, and he did not doubt his father's assessment one bit. He imagined a scene of smoke and fire and bayonets flashing, ear-splitting noises, screams, the cracking of tree branches shattered by the salvos of musket shot. Over in two minutes. A skirmish, probably unrecorded in the history of the war between the states. An accidental encounter between two squadrons trying at all costs to avoid one another. The battle meant nothing, really, to the war. But everything to the bones below.

"Are you okay, Dad?"

His father looked at him straight on; the slackness of his face had disappeared. For a second, Clayton recognized him as the man he once was.

"It will come out right."

"How can I help? I don't know what to do."

"You sit here with me a while. Then we get up, you and I, and we go about our business."

"There's more to it than that."

"There's no more. You got to handle your life, I got to

handle mine."

"There's nothing to handle with mine. It don't amount to nothing yet. I got time for you, if you let me."

"I feel the sadness below this ground. I feel sadness in you, too. You got troubles, and you don't need more from me."

They sat there in silence as the day ebbed. The light weakened and then began to fade. The lessening breeze creaked through the trees; a squirrel rustled the deadfall. Toward dusk, a white-tailed deer emerged cautiously from a thicket and foraged in the opening. The sound of a dog barking far off startled it back into the undergrowth.

"Let's get on home," his father said and rose from the hummock. "Momma will be getting worried."

Clayton followed his father back through the woods. He had not felt so close to him since before he'd left for the war.

▶ ▶ ▶

Clayton helped his mother with the dishes after dinner while his father sat watching television, some variety show with singing acts and comedians and dogs playing a baseball game. From the kitchen, Clayton could hear the audience howl with laughter. He glanced out at his father, who stared stone-faced into the screen.

"He make it to work regular?"

"'Course he does, just like I told you. He'd never let himself sit idle."

"You two doing okay, the bills and all?"

"My goodness, what a question. 'Course we are."

"Because I have a little set aside. You're welcome to it."

His mother stiffened noticeably. "Listen to you. You think your father can't take care of us? Don't be silly. We're just fine."

They washed and dried the dinnerware while Clayton's mother went on about the family that had moved in next door—"Papists, you know"— and the man at the grocery store who had just hired a Negro to run the produce department. It was the talk of the neighborhood, and in passing, she added something about Clayton's room all fixed for him and that, "Oh, by the way, I called Mr. Whitehead down at the lumberyard while you and your father were out, and he said they were looking for a few hands, and, yes, he would be right happy to talk to you."

Late that night, Clayton lay in bed staring up at the ceiling, listening to the night sounds, a truck far off, the house creaking under its own weight. He was a hundred and six miles from the coast, he had clocked it on the odometer, yet he swore he could hear the surf against the beach, the rhythmic washing of gentle waves, not a pounding, but almost a caressing of sea to sand, a lulling that would normally ease him to sleep but tonight only tormented him.

In the night's darkest hour, around three, he guessed, Clayton rose from bed and turned on the nightstand lamp. He retrieved his wallet from the top of the dresser, removed a hundred dollars in twenty-dollar bills, and tucked the money beneath his pillow. Then he packed his duffel and he made his bed—he would not want his mother to be more offended than she would be anyway—and he crept downstairs.

His father sat in the recliner, smoking in the dark. Clayton could see the red tip of the cigarette and could make out his dim outline from the weak wash of the porch light.

"Have a safe journey, Son."

"Dad, I'm so sorry. I have to go."

"Of course you do."

"If you asked, I'd stay."

"I know you would. I'd never do that."

"Dad, if I could help … "

"Go on, Son. Go on out. I'll explain to Momma. Son?"

"Yes, Dad?"

"You make me proud, boy."

"Don't say that. Please don't. I could tell you things."

"You make me proud. You are a man, and I had something to do with that, and you are strong enough to go on and make your own life."

"Tell Mom I'll call when I get settled."

▶ ▶ ▶

Into the midlands, he thought. Thirty-seven dollars to carry him, the sum total of his fortune, not counting loose change. He had seen pictures of Iowa, Illinois, the flat, green expanses, and he thought nothing could be farther from the sea. But he was wrong. Even inland, the broad plains, the crops waving in the breeze, the far horizon reminded him of a gentle swell on the bay. So he continued west. He slept in his car at the side of the road and ate sparingly, only one real meal a day. The Plymouth guzzled fuel and lost oil like blood seeping from an open wound, a quart a day, and it gave out in Kansas along a stretch of country road somewhere between Salina and Hays. He stood beside the car, steam and smoke billowing from beneath its hood, and looked out across section after section of ripening corn. His line of sight carried to a windbreak two miles out at least, and with the flat expanse of farmland before him and the unbroken blue of the sky above, he had never felt so exposed and vulnerable before, not even when he had been alone in his small boat on the Chesapeake. He fought the urge to duck into the field, to grub between the furrows, to crawl underneath his car, but, instead, he put one foot in front of the other and continued west, away from his broken-down hulk and this open land that reminded him too much of the sea.

A trucker freighting hogs gave him a ride and bought him lunch. Late at night, after the highway traffic slowed to almost nothing, he slept in a gully and felt lonely and shabbily transient. At twenty-three, worthless.

The following day, in Sterling, Colorado, he was hitching by the side of the highway when a Cadillac convertible slowed and pulled onto the shoulder ahead of him. A man sat behind the wheel with a fifth of Jack Daniels wedged between his legs. His hair was long and wavy, reminding Clayton a little of one of those new rock-and-roll stars, and he wore a white shirt studded with pearl buttons and a leather string tie clasped by a turquoise stone the size of a gull's egg.

"You know how to drive, boy?"

"I do."

"Then come on around here. I been out joyriding from Denver. Think I need a little rest."

The man climbed from the car and walked around the back of it and got into the passenger seat. Clayton tossed his duffel into the rear seat and slid behind the wheel and drove on. He had never been in a car like this before—the smooth red leather upholstery still holding the smell of newness, the sleek white body without mar or dent and gleaming in the morning sun as he raced it across the high plains. The man beside him was soon asleep, head back, snoring, the bottle slipped to the floor. Clayton felt the dry wind on his face, tousling his hair. The radio blasted doo-wop, and for a moment, he knew if not happiness, then at least an absence of despair.

In the distance, the mountains slowly grew from the horizon like huge ocean swells. July, and snow still capped the peaks. Clayton recognized that they could swallow up a man and knew he would travel straight into the middle of them. He came up on the city of Denver, a hazy oddity of office towers and stockyards and converging rail tracks planted at the very edge of the foothills. The owner of the Cadillac slept on, so Clayton continued driving west, past hogbacks that reminded him of the armor plates of a stegosaurus, then, downshifting, up into the mountains. Even in July, the air was cool, and the sleeping man unconsciously crossed his arms and snorted once. An hour into high country, the road pleated into a series of switchbacks that traversed the side of a mountain. Clayton's progress was slowed by a logging truck creeping uphill. The whining of the truck's engine finally woke the sleeping man, who sat up in his seat, massaged his temples with his thumb and forefinger, and looked about him in temporary confusion.

"Where the hell are we?"

"Don't know exactly."

"Well, shit-fire, boy, we're up in the goddamn mountains."

"I guess."

"Pull over. Pull over, and get on out of the goddamn car."

They approached the summit of the pass, and Clayton eased the car to the shoulder of the road, precariously close to the downhill slope. Clayton exited the car and walked around to retrieve his bag from the backseat passenger side. They were above tree line, and Clayton looked down the mountainside to where a few scarred spruces fought up from the boulder-studded earth. A raven took flight from one of the trees and glided above a talus slide. The man had climbed over the stick shift, settled into the driver's seat, and was now attempting a U-turn on the narrow road but was blocked by the uphill side of the mountain. Clayton watched as he backed up and finally completed the turn.

"You're in the middle of nowhere, boy. Got plans?"

"Where this road lead to?"

"Pretty much what you're looking at now. A few mined-out towns. Not much else."

The man pulled away, and Clayton started walking, but soon another logging truck appeared and gave him a lift down into the valley.

four

Nora's Café occupied a glass-fronted brick building along Main Street in the three-block town of Peakview. There were two taverns enclosing the town's outskirts like parentheses, a church steeple poking up from one of the side arteries, a small grocery, a hardware, and a sporting-goods store with a Hunters Welcome sign hanging over the entrance even though it was midsummer, months before any hunting season opened. The namesake peak rose dramatically to the west of town and threw Main Street into shadow for much of the day.

When Clayton entered the café, it was crowded. The tables had been pushed against the walls, and people squeezed into the perimeter window booths while others stood in the cleared center of the room and faced the far wall, where a man in a suit pointed to an easel that held what looked like an aerial map. Two state troopers flanked him. Clayton hung back near the entryway and watched.

The man in the suit pointed to the dark line of the river snaking through the valley. "Here," he said. "This is where we'll begin the diversion. The dam will go here. This area," he circled the town with his pointer, "will be the reservoir."

"That area," an angry voice shot back, "is our town!"

"You know we've been planning this for years. You've had notice. You'll be compensated fairly."

"How you going to compensate my son, my grandson, who won't have the ranch no more? How you going to do that?"

"This reservoir will be a boon to this town. You can rebuild over here, on the eastern shore. Tourists will drive up to boat, fish."

"You didn't answer me."

"There's land enough out here to ranch. Acres available near Rangeley, Meeker. You have plenty of time to locate a new spread."

"But not in the valley. Never again in the valley."

After the meeting, the men moved the tables back into the middle of the room and filtered out of the café. Clayton took a stool at the counter and watched them leave. They stood talking in small groups outside. Someone passed a pint. Clayton watched and pained for the strangers. He knew what it was like to be uprooted.

In the midafternoon lull, only one booth remained occupied following the town meeting: two older women were having pie and coffee. Three other red vinyl booths lined the walls, and, including the Formica tables, the small room could seat perhaps twenty-five. The smell of frying hamburger and onion hung in the air. Clayton studied the one-page mimeographed menu, weighing his empty stomach against his equally empty pockets.

The waitress behind the counter placed a glass

of water in front of him and leaned both hands on the counter. "What can I get you?"

She appeared to be closing on middle age, a little older than Sonny, maybe, with a sturdy build, solid, a body without loose folds. A swath of dark hair streaked with premature white had escaped from her bun and hung limply down the side of her face. Her hands were large, with wrists almost as thick as Clayton's. But her face was friendly—a slightly upturned mouth, inquisitive, alert eyes.

"A grilled cheese, maybe. With tomato. And coffee."

"Fries?"

"No, thanks."

The woman tucked her hair back into her bun. She walked to the grill and began to assemble his sandwich. She called over her shoulder to the two women sitting in the booth, "How you two doing over there? More coffee?"

One of the women answered, "No, we are just fine," and shortly afterward, they slid out of the booth and left.

When they opened the front door, Clayton felt a sharp gust against his face and noticed the wind kicking up a dust swirl in front of the stores lining the opposite side of the road. Main Street was paved, but, as far as he could tell, the side roads were all dirt and gravel.

He got up and walked to the bathroom at the rear of the diner to wash his face and hands, and when he returned, the grilled-cheese sandwich was on the counter along with some fried potatoes and a slab of berry pie. The waitress stood by the cash register thumbing through the morning's receipts.

"Left over from the lunch rush. Just have to toss it if you can't eat it."

"Thank you."

Clayton ate in silence and chewed slowly, a trick he had learned traveling across country. Made a little seem like more.

The waitress cleaned the vacated booth and scraped down the grill with the edge of a spatula. When she came to refill his coffee cup, Clayton looked up.

"Are you Nora?"

"I am."

"Sign in your window says you could use some help."

She regarded him. "With that accent of yours, I figured you were new here, either passing through or looking for work. Can you fry cook?"

"Not yet."

"Well, that's a honest answer. Drink? Last one I had to finally let go. A decent fella, steady when he was sober, but the bottle just got the best of him. The story of a lot of lives around here."

"I can't afford to drink much."

"Why not get on with the mines up valley? You look

to have ten fingers and ten toes. They're hiring, and the pay is good."

"I don't much like the idea of going down in a hole."

"Take your choice around here. Down in a hole, sure. But still some placer mining on the streams, small-time operators. And surface mining too, for hard rock."

Clayton sampled the pie. "I saw what they are doing to that mountain. That work doesn't much appeal to me either."

Coming into the valley, Clayton had noticed a hacked-down twin to the town's peak, with one side staved in like a cancer had been carved out of it. Weather-beaten trailers dotted the land around the mining operation, and a gauze of smoke draped the entire conglomeration of housing and machinery.

"Have it your way," Nora said. "Here, the pay's bad and the hours are worse. We pretty much cater to the mine and the ranch schedules. And the construction crews, lately. Open at five, gets busy right away. Then again from eleven to two, and five to seven. I close after the lunch hour on Saturday and all day Sunday."

"That sounds just fine by me. Thanks." Clayton stood and pulled a few wadded dollar bills from his pocket.

Nora shook her head. "Food comes with the job. What you call a perk. Great benefit package here at Nora's."

When she smiled, he thought she looked years

younger.

Clayton left Nora's Café and walked up Main Street toward the sporting-goods store. With what money he had left, he thought to buy a sweatshirt for what he expected would be the cool mountain nights. Men were still huddled in tight knots up and down the street. One of the men partially blocked the door.

"Excuse me," Clayton said.

"You new here?" the man asked.

He looked at Clayton with something like a challenge. Within spitting distance of Clayton's age, the man was stocky, barrel-chested, but a little soft around the middle. He wore a sweat-stained felt work hat, brim curled in front, flat and turned down in the back. *A real cowboy hat*, Clayton thought, *a real cowboy. But a little soft.*

"I am. Clayton Royster." He stuck out his hand.

The man ignored it. "Goddamn construction," he said and spat on the sidewalk.

"No, fry cook," Clayton said. "Over to Nora's."

"Don't look like no fry cook."

A second man, same age as the first, bone thin, with a beaklike nose and dull eyes, studied his friend with confusion. He removed the green cap from his head and scratched his scalp. "Duane, what is a fry cook supposed to look like?"

"Not like him. Hell, look at him. He talks funny. He's

got no hat on his head. He just don't fit in at all."

"I see that," the other man said. "It's just that I don't know if that makes him a fry cook or a goddamn construction worker or what."

A third man added, "He's what you might call a conundrum."

The others turned to the man with bewilderment.

"I tell you what," Clayton said. "You all let me know when you got it all talked out, but right now, I got business inside."

He waited for Duane to step aside. Duane appeared in no hurry to comply.

"You boys quit tormenting this man." This from an older man who had walked up behind Clayton, a man who spoke with authority and had a deep, level voice. "I know you fellas got better use of your time than holding down the sidewalk."

"Yes, sir, Mac. It's just that we know how you feel about them people come into the valley to take your land."

"Why don't you let me worry about my land? Go on now."

Clayton and Mac watched the men drive off in two pickups.

"Name's Hoyt McKnight," the old man said and shook hands with Clayton. "You'll have to excuse those boys. They've been nipping a bit after the meeting. The one, Duane, he's a mean drinker. I use them some on the ranch. They aren't much as hands go, but help's short and you end up hiring on who you can."

"There was some tension at that meeting," Clayton said.

"There's some people been here a long time," Mac said. "Feelings run deep."

"I heard you in there," Clayton said. He remembered Mac's anger, his booming voice.

Mac pointed up to the mountain. "Named after my daddy," he said. "Mount McKnight. People hike it in the summer after snowmelt. A wondrous view from the summit."

Clayton looked up at the peak. It seemed impossibly remote. "How they get up there?" he asked.

"There's a trail. Nothing technical. Just got to be in walking shape."

They both stared up at the summit for a bit, as if contemplating a hike, then Mac spoke again.

"Eminent domain. Eminent domain, they call it. I call it murder. Take a man's life right out from under him."

"What's to be done?" Clayton asked.

"Probably nothing," Mac answered. "But when the time comes, I'll have to take a stand. Could not live with myself otherwise."

Clayton shook his head in sympathy and looked down

the street. An anvil thunderhead rose over the mountain. He noticed Nora close up the café and walk away from them. Maybe Mac had been at the whiskey also. Probably. Because men do not often speak from their heart, as Mac seemed to be. It was not in their nature. But it made Clayton feel suddenly close to him, a conspirator of sorts. Clayton himself held it all in as much as he could, and he admired someone who could occasionally let it out.

"Well," Mac said, "nice to meet you, Son. Welcome to our little drama of a town—for as long as it lasts, anyway. Let me know if those yahoos bother you, and I'll have a talk with them."

"Appreciate it, but I expect I'll be just fine."

▸ ▸ ▸

Clayton lived out the summer in a tent on the slopes behind town. Often during those first months, he hiked to the summit of Mount McKnight. It was indeed a wondrous view. To the west, the Rockies stretched out beyond vision, snow holding stubbornly in the pleats and folds of the mountains. To the east, through a notch in the Front Range, he could make out where the land flattened into prairie, blue in the distance, passing into infinity. It reminded him of the ocean, all of this vast openness, and, by association, Loretta Pine, and he would go weak-kneed with shame, at the sight of Loretta's voluntary humiliation and his role in it. He would stand there and shudder with fervor, literally shaking the image from his memory, and then he would hike back down the mountain and would not talk to anyone for a few days.

A month after he had settled in Peakview, Clayton fed twelve quarters into the pay phone at the back of the café and dialed a long-distance number. After three rings, the other line was picked up.

"Hello, Sonny."

"It's good to hear your voice. You okay, boy?"

"I am. Listen, Sonny, I need you do something for me. Collect my gear, my boats and equipment, and sell it all off."

There was a pause at the other end, and then Sonny spoke. "Where you at, Son?"

"Out West. I'm done with the water, Sonny. I'm as far from it as I can get."

"Why you run off like you did? Thought you and Walter was going to talk things out."

"Didn't work out that way. I'm done with it. Done with it all."

"If I sell the gear, where you want me to send the money?"

"You keep it. I don't need the money."

"Then I won't sell your boat, Clayton. I won't sell the crab pots. I'll store them up for you. I got room."

"I won't be back, Sonny."

"Still, I'll not end it like that."

"Do what you want. Burn them, for all I care."

"You're talking crazy now. Just settle down for a bit and get your sense back and then we can talk some more."

"One more thing, Sonny. Could you get this number to my folks? They can reach me here."

"You want me to give them a call, see if things are okay?"

"Thanks. You take care, hear? I'll be talking to you."

Clayton hung up the phone. He knew he would not be able to ask about Loretta but thought at least he would feel better after giving up his boat. Something decided. Something let go. Instead, his insides felt empty, and he left to fill them up with beer.

▶ ▶ ▶

With the first tentative snows of September, Nora put down a mattress on the floor of the storeroom and brought in a table and chair. "It's not much," she motioned to the room, "but it's warm. I wouldn't want my fry cook froze solid by a quick storm. Wouldn't be able to pry you from the ground until spring."

Clayton noticed a stack of winter clothing neatly folded on the table: long underwear, a pair of flannel trousers, two sweaters, a heavy wool coat. He held up the coat, appreciating its heft.

"Thought you could use them. He was about your size."

"Your husband?"

She nodded.

"Where's he now?"

"Gone. He was a trucker. Still is. Loved the road, to be on the move."

"And you?"

"I used to travel with him some. But I never took to it. The town grew on me. I bought the café, and that kept me home. After one trip, four years now, he just decided he wouldn't be coming back."

"Sounds like a hard man."

"No, not at all. Neither of us did anything wrong. Nothing spiteful. We loved each other. Then we didn't. We just drifted apart."

"It's good you can be done and just move on with life."

Nora reached out and caressed the jacket that Clayton held. "Sometimes I still mourn," she said, not looking at Clayton any longer but at the jacket, running her hand down along one sleeve. "He was a good man," she said, and turned from the room.

Clayton lay awake long into the night. He had wanted

to ask Nora more, how she managed. To love and then not to. To get by when it was over. To mourn only sometimes. To get through even one day without that old yearning coming on swift and painful and without warning, like a heart attack.

By December, weather swept into the valley, sealing it off from the rest of civilization for days at a time. During the third week in January that first year, a great storm blew in. Midday on a Tuesday, Clayton stood at the door and watched the snow fall so heavily that he lost sight of the hardware store directly across the street from Nora's, no more than twenty yards distant. Road traffic slowed, the occasional truck drifting by like a shadow, like a ghost ship, and by evening, the streets were deserted. They closed the café early, and, with Nora at home, Clayton sat by himself in a window booth marveling at the quiet force of the storm continuing to build outside.

Sometime during the night, the power failed and the wind picked up and drifted the snow above the window of the café and blocked the door completely. For two days, Clayton was alone in the restaurant. He made coffee on the gas stove and sat in one of the booths drinking and reading by the dim glow of light that filtered in through the snow banking the windows. It was a place of exquisite exile so foreign to his experience that it seemed a different world entirely, a different reality, a hibernation, and he could feel his blood slowing, his body suspended in a long, soft exhale, and he forgot for a while his remembrances of home, his disgrace, his sense of abandonment both of Loretta and of his parents, so that the weight lifted temporarily from his soul. He experienced in a way something like his father's withdrawal from the life around him, and he realized it could be a release of sorts, liberation rather than imprisonment.

He was disappointed when he heard the plows working outside, and even before the roads were cleared from this latest storm, he looked forward to the next.

▶ ▶ ▶

One Saturday in mid-February, Clayton was cleaning the grill as the last of the noontime customers filed out.

Nora wiped down the counter and came over to him. "Take a walk with me this afternoon?" she asked.

"Sure. Where to?"

"A place I want to show you. Dress warm. Bring your snowshoes."

The day was clear and cold, a pale sun descending from its zenith, a sky so blue, it lacked dimension.

They hiked out of town on the main road then paused to strap on their snowshoes before continuing on a trail into the woods that blanketed the mountain slope. They climbed through aspen groves, white and stark, like skeletons. The trees cast shadows on the snow, black tendrils reaching for them as they passed through the groves and up into the pines. They did not talk. The hike demanded their attention, the trail marked by green metal tags nailed to the trees every hundred yards or so. The snow was deep, the forest thick, and they both understood the perils of losing their way. Clayton listened to the sounds of the forest, snow squeaking beneath their feet, trees groaning against the cold. He breathed deeply with the exertion and noted the clean, almost-lifeless scent of this country; there was a subtle fragrance of the pine but little else, as if the thin air could support only its own essence. The air lacked the humidity of home, a humidity that carried with it unmistakable hints of seaweed and salt and assorted wildlife, dead and alive.

In time, the trail leveled and the forest opened into a pocket of meadow perhaps fifty yards across. Clayton followed Nora to the far end where the land fell steeply away and offered a view of the town below. It spread out in miniature: playhouses lining Main Street, toy cars dark against the snow-packed road, tin figures gliding into and out of the buildings. Beyond town, the valley stretched out, the river frozen and glinting in the late sun, snaking its way through a notch in the range at the western limit of the basin.

"We used to come up here," Nora said. "Camp in the

summer. Watch the lights of town come on and then go off. The darker the town got, the night sky just opened up. Stars so thick, they looked like they were woven together into a blanket. Like a blanket you could just reach up to and wrap yourself in."

Nora seemed to be in another place, another time, and Clayton just looked off across the valley and let her talk.

"Then in the morning—moon still hanging above the mountains over there, sun in the east. Wood smoke rising from town. And we're up here in a different world, just watching it all. Like gods."

They stood in silence for a few minutes, then Nora gave her head a shake. "We'd best get back down the hill while there's still light enough to follow our track."

"Thanks for showing me this place," Clayton said. "It's beautiful."

"It's someplace I thought you'd like. And I needed to see it today."

▶ ▶ ▶

A week later, Clayton had a few beers at one of the bars and returned to the café early and went directly to his mattress in the storeroom and slept deeply. Sometime during the middle of the night, a sound brought him groggily awake, and he heard a voice.

"It's me."

He rolled onto his back and in the dim light from the streetlamps could make out Nora's silhouette.

"Can I stay a while?"

"You want me to make coffee?"

"No. I want to come lie beside you. Would that be all right?"

Clayton heard something in her voice, a calm desperation that would have made him agree with anything at all that she asked at that moment. "Yes."

Clayton turned onto his side, away from her, and listened to the rustle of her clothes falling away and felt the weight of her body lowered onto the mattress and then the incredible warmth of her as she pressed her length against his back. Heavy breasts, taught nipples, her leg raised across his hip, the tight curls of her pubic hair scratching against the hump of his buttocks. They rested there, silent, Clayton not sure what to do, until he thought perhaps she had fallen asleep. But then her hands gently moved over him, his chest, the concavity of his stomach, his penis, and he felt her lips brushing his shoulder blades, her tongue sampling here and there, and he felt himself coming alive for the first time in months, and he turned to face her.

▸ ▸ ▸

Sunday morning, with the café closed for the day, Clayton

rose early while Nora slept, and he made coffee and eggs and fried a slab of ham. Presently, she appeared beside him, fully dressed and holding her coat.

"Coffee's ready. Eggs in a minute."

"None for me. I have to be going."

Clayton turned to her. "Last night … ," he started, but did not know where to take the conversation.

"I thank you for last night," Nora said.

"It's me should thank you."

"No. There's some dates that are hard for me to get through. Yesterday was one of them, and you helped more than you know."

She went to the door, and suddenly Clayton felt desperate to keep open some possibility that he could not articulate. "Come to me again, when you need to. Will you?"

Nora smiled at him and left.

▶ ▶ ▶

He lasted in the café until spring. The weather turned, and he felt drawn to the outdoors like water during the ebbing tide drawn back to sea. Nora sensed his restlessness.

"Saw Hoyt the other day at the hardware," she told him one raw April morning.

Outside, rain and snow mixed, and people in the café nursed their last cups of coffee.

"Said he's having a hell of a time finding help for the ranch."

"He still have Jesse and Duane with him?"

"When they got nothing better to do. He said the two of them together added up to about a half-day's work. That's when they're on top of their game."

"Seems a fair man. Wonder why he can't get help."

"You're still new here, so you wouldn't notice, but people's been leaving the valley. That dam is still years from being finished, but people see the future. They see it right in front of their eyes, the earthmovers, bulldozers. It's starting. They're taking their buyouts and moving on. This café's down. Business is down all over. Truth is, Mac doesn't need full-time help either. Still running a few head, growing some feed, just to be obstinate, mainly."

Clayton cleared the last of the breakfast dishes and washed them. Nora put aside the syrup and the honey jars and set out ketchup and mustard.

"You should go see him," Nora said when they were finished setting up for lunch.

"I couldn't leave you here without help," Clayton said.

"Things are slow here most weekdays, you know that. I could still use you on weekends, but you'd have time for both. Get you outdoors, get a little color back to your hide."

▶ ▶ ▶

Mac gave Clayton the old foreman's cabin to stay in on the days he helped at the ranch. It was sided in unfinished lumber, had one room with a bed and a few pegs on the wall for his clothes. It had a bare plank floor and no plumbing. But Mac had run an electric line in some years back, the iron stove kept the place warm and the coffee hot, and the cabin had a covered porch where Clayton could sit most evenings as night came on.

The work itself Clayton loved. Mac had moved the majority of his herd to acreage he owned around Meeker, but he kept a few head on the ranch to remind himself that he was a cattleman, and he insisted the homestead be kept in working order. Clayton stayed busy mending fences and clearing out the drainage ditches. Mac attempted to teach him to properly sit a horse, but the act of climbing onto a large animal's back seemed unnatural to Clayton. The few times he and Mac rode together proved an irritation to both. Mac had to rein in constantly to wait on Clayton, who thought he was already riding at an uncomfortable pace, his ass slamming against the saddle, his shoulders tense. By the time they reached the herd or some water pump that needed repair, Clayton was already exhausted, whereas Mac felt impatient with the dawdling pace of their commute. They both quickly realized that Clayton belonged behind the wheel of the old farm pickup and that work with the animals was best left to the few locals still around and willing to be hired out. From his time at the gas station with Sonny, Clayton had developed an instinctive understanding of machinery, and he proved valuable in keeping the assortment of ancient contraptions in working order—the mowers, three trucks, all dating from before Clayton's birth, the pumps and generators and compressors that seemed a ubiquitous presence on a working ranch. On weekends and Wednesday evenings, he continued to help Nora at the café.

On occasion, Mac had Clayton up to the main house. After dinner, they made a habit of going out front to sip whiskey and look out over the valley. Mac would talk of the early days.

"My daddy settled here in '77. I was born in the ranch house in '85, lived here all my life. Remodeled some, added plumbing and whatnot, but the central beams, most of the planking, I kept from the old place. I remember when the Ute still came up to hunt elk in the fall. They'd bring their whole families, camp in the pastures. We'd listen to them around their fires at night."

The old man seemed to drift back in time for a moment. Listening to him, Clayton could imagine the land during those early days, open and wide and empty.

"I used to go out on the sand at night sometimes," Clayton told of his own home. "Sit and stare out at the ocean, the moon off the water. It just went on forever.

Endless. I still got saltwater in my veins, but I sometimes get that same feeling here, looking out. Like home."

Mac listened to Clayton, then they both fell silent. A coyote sounded in the hills. Then another.

Mac said, "Wait here. I got something to show you." He disappeared into the house and returned a few minutes later holding a rock. "What do you see here?"

Clayton examined the rock Mac handed him, held it up to catch the moonlight. "Why, it's a shell of some kind. In the rock. A fossil?"

"I found it up on the mountain one day. In an old worked-out quarry. Never told anyone. Don't need more outsiders poking around up here. That there fossil is why you feel something here. This place used to be sea. It's the sea in these hills that drew you. It's the sea that will call you back home, sooner or later."

▶ ▶ ▶

The seasons passed. One year, then another. Clayton settled into his solitude as if he had been born to it. He indulged in a Saturday-night beer or two at one of the taverns, exchanging congenial if impersonal conversation, what mine had played out, market prices at the stockyard, who was selling, who was buying. But that was as close as he came to friendship.

Every few months, he would check in with Sonny,

sometimes just to hear the accent of home. He never asked about Loretta, and Sonny never offered news of her. They talked mostly of the water. In the years Clayton had been gone, striped bass had almost disappeared from the bay. Crabbing was down, then up again, an ebb and flow of fortunes almost like the tide itself. Clayton would keep Sonny on the phone as long as he could afford to feed quarters into the black box, keep him talking about the sea until he could almost remember the smell of salt in the air.

Five or six times a year, Nora would visit him at night. An anniversary date, he imagined, a birthday. He almost never sought her out, waiting for her to come to him, even though some nights he lay in bed filled with his own lone-liness, his own anniversaries, willing her to appear. When he would finally drop off to sleep, however, it would be Loretta, not Nora, who came to him in his dreams, and he would wake up muzzy with guilt.

Only once had Clayton sought Nora's comfort on his own initiative. It was March of 1959. Early one morning, the phone at the café roused Clayton from his storeroom bunk. As he walked out front to answer the call, he noticed fine snow reflecting in the streetlight. *No sun today*, he thought. *Mud season late in coming this year.* He picked up the receiver, and Sonny's voice came over a line filled with static and breaks. Perhaps it was the poor connection, but his accent sounded to Clayton thicker and more drawn than he had remembered, almost foreign. Suddenly, Virginia seemed very distant, a world and an age away.

"Hey, boy, I got some news for you."

"Hey, Sonny."

"The old man," Sonny said, and then the line crackled and Clayton missed the next few sentences.

"Say again, Sonny. Can hardly hear you."

"The old man," Sonny repeated, "Walter Pine, he died."

"Died? Did I hear right?"

"Stroke or some such. Not mourned around these parts. Only a few at his service."

"I appreciate the news, Sonny. I hadn't really thought about him in a long while."

There was quiet on the other line, and Clayton thought maybe they had been disconnected.

Then Sonny came back on. "You don't usually lie to me, Son. It ain't a becoming trait."

"Really, Sonny, my life's here now."

"No reason it needs to be. You could be home."

"This is as much home as I need."

"There you go again. Let me tell you about the girl, Loretta."

And then the line did go dead. Clayton tapped the black receiver against the wall, held it to his ear. Nothing—dead air, not even a dial tone. Storm must have knocked down a line again.

So … news he had been dreaming about for years. What of it? He had no rights. Home—what was that? A girl he felt he had disgraced—and she'd turned from him also that day. Chose the store, the security. She was somebody there; people respected her, he imagined. She was the wife of a store owner, someone to be considered. He had left his parents in their time of need. Was that home? Abandoned his parents, abandoned his girl, abandoned his dream of a life on the sea. And given it up for what? Fry cook in a dead-end mountain town. He was angry, then afraid, then terrified as he felt some of his father's dark shadow creep into his soul. He worked his shift that day in silence, and Nora noticed something about him, some burden. Before she left for the day, she caressed his arm in passing. No words, just a gentle touch. Later that evening, he knocked on her front door, and she drew him to her. He had never asked Sonny about Loretta.

Over time, a warm tenderness developed between the two of them, Nora and Clayton, two people biding time until life could again gain purchase within them—or not. They understood this about each other, and it was a bond of sorts, a comfort, but their unshared secrecies precluded real intimacy. He never traded his storeroom mattress for a more permanent and personal residence, and Nora never pushed him, though now and again she tried to convince him that life had more to give than he was taking. He always listened politely and went on about his business.

▶ ▶ ▶

In 1963, Nora bought a television for the café. Her customers liked to watch the news and comment on the crazy happenings in the outside world as if they were actually a part of it. Clayton watched too, but felt no sense of belonging at all. Even when a president was assassinated, he felt as if some swirling kaleidoscope were filling his vision with a geometry of dark and murky images that held no reality for him.

Despite the addition of the television, business at the café gradually slowed as the years ticked off because the town was dying, literally. Living on borrowed time. For the past three years, topographic teams had been surveying and drilling bore holes. The diversion tunnels were blasted to redirect the river around the dam site, and now construction crews were replacing miners in Nora's café. By the end of 1964, few of the old-timers remained.

"I'm not relocating down valley," Nora told him one day in early spring as they were closing for the evening. "I'm not starting over up here," she said.

Earlier that week, she had accepted the water board's

final buyout offer and had been given a vacancy date.

"I'm taking myself down the hill into Denver. Drink some of that water that's so important to them. Two showers a day. Maybe look into opening a diner or a coffee shop."

"I just might be ready for Denver too," Clayton said. "Maybe help you get settled."

"No, Clayton," she said, and placed a hand lightly on his shoulder. "There's holes in both of us that need mending. But I don't think we can help each other with the patching. It's time for a new start. Time for you too."

Clayton scraped down the grill and ran a wet cloth over it. The grill steamed and hissed. "I'll give it some thought," he said.

"Don't think on it too long," she said, her voice soft and tender. "You need to take a look in the mirror. Neither of us is getting any younger."

Clayton had turned thirty-one that winter.

▶ ▶ ▶

A week later, Clayton was mopping the floor after lunch when a commotion out front caught his attention. A group of men were in animated conversation. He walked outside.

"Drove him off. Stood in the road with his rifle."

"What happened?" Clayton asked.

"They went to serve Mac an eviction notice. He turned them back. Sheriff and three people from the state."

"Where's he now? Mac?"

"Still at the ranch."

Clayton walked back into the diner and hung his apron on the hook inside the front door and left for the ranch. At the turnoff from the main road, the sheriff's brown patrol car blocked the entrance.

The sheriff waved him down as he turned in. "Road's closed."

"My gear is up there," Clayton answered. "At the cabin."

Clayton and the sheriff knew each other in passing, but neither seemed inclined to extend further greetings.

"Police business. You can't get through. I don't need complications."

Clayton drove the ranch truck around the bend and pulled off to the shoulder and parked. He cut through the field to the ranch. He found Mac struggling with bales of hay, stacking them three high in a line across the road. A 12-gauge shotgun rested on top of one of the bales. Clayton set about helping to stack the hay. They worked in silence for twenty minutes until they had constructed a barricade in a semicircle around the front of the ranch house.

"No need for you to be here," Mac said.

"I didn't know they'd served notice on you."

"Been getting legal papers in the mail. Knew it was coming."

They were both sweating, but the sun was lowering and already the day was cooling. They walked inside and got a beer from the icebox and sat on the front porch as the day waned. At nightfall, mule deer moved from the pines into the fields. Neither of the men felt like eating. They just sat and watched the deer until they melted into the dark.

"I have a son and a daughter, did you know that?"

"No."

"One in Phoenix, one in L.A. Know what they want to do with the ranch house?"

"No."

"Cut it right down the middle. Move each section up the hill there, where the lakeshore will be after the reservoir is finished. Splice them back together and turn the place into a resort. A dude ranch. My daddy's homestead, a dude ranch."

Clayton could feel the disappointment in Mac's voice.

"It's not just about my ranch."

"I know."

"It's the land. The way of things in this valley."

"Yes."

"I'm not a fool."

"No, sir, you are not."

"I can't stop the change. I know that. But I can't have this place just plucked up and moved like a circus tent. I won't have it turned into a damned motel for the rich folk to play cowboy. And I sure as hell won't watch them bulldoze it."

Then Mac breathed deeply, taking in the night air, and Clayton sensed that he might be trying to draw the history of this place into his body, into his soul.

"Help me?" Mac asked.

"Yes, sir."

They rose from the porch step, and Clayton waited while Mac walked out to the truck and pulled two gas cans from the bed and handed one to Clayton. Clayton followed him back inside. They doused the bedding upstairs and the couch and stuffed chairs in the front rooms downstairs. Mac opened the gas lines on the stove. Back on the porch, Mac lit an oil rag and without hesitation tossed it inside. They drove to the foreman's cabin and sat in the cab of the pickup watching the flames lick from the windows until finally the rafters took and the kitchen stove blew with a swoosh that shot flames through the open front door.

▶ ▶ ▶

By May of 1965, construction on the dam neared completion and the town sat all but abandoned in the river valley waiting for the reservoir to engulf it. Clayton packed the last of Nora's boxes into the bed of her pickup and stood leaning against the cab, staring off down the vacant main street. Nora had wanted a few minutes alone in the café but now came out.

"Funny," she said, "how without the customers, without the smell of meals cooking, it just doesn't feel that hard to walk away from."

"You've put in a lot of years there."

"I don't regret giving it up. I'm ready to move on."

"That's good."

"Listen," she said suddenly and grabbed Clayton's arm. She had begun to speak, then just pursed her lips, as if she were locking the words away, then tried to speak again. "I worry about you," she finally said. "Don't stay here. I don't know what you're looking for, but it's not here. You are not of this place."

"You've been a good friend. No—more than that. Thanks."

They both looked away, eyes scanning the streets, then off to the mountains that enclosed the valley, to the peaks that held the white gold that was the area's future.

"Well," Nora said and climbed in behind the wheel.

"You take care," Clayton said.

"You got the keys to the café?" Nora asked and then

laughed. "I guess there's no need to lock up after you leave."

She started the truck and pulled away, and Clayton watched her until she turned onto the main highway and disappeared around a curve, and he stood there for a long while staring at the empty road.

Is it that easy? Clayton thought. *To have and to let go? What is wrong with me?*

Clayton stayed in the café that spring as the remaining shops emptied and the townspeople moved on. The bars were the last to close, but by June, even they had been vacated, and Clayton spent his days observing the construction crew excavating the borrow pits for the raw materials to finish off the dam. The demolition team rumbled into town, leveling the buildings from the outskirts inward. When the crews left for the day, he sat on the steps of the café and listened to the town—the heaped ruins of the bulldozed buildings settling in creaks and moans, the breeze flapping the advertising banner hanging in shreds from a single support beam planted beside the skeleton of the sporting-goods store. One evening at dusk, a coyote stalked down the center of Main Street, as if reclaiming it. The stillness, the desolate calm reminded Clayton of the salt bay. He wondered if Loretta felt this alone.

When summer came to the valley, the café was in the demolition crew's path, so Clayton moved to the overlook that Nora had shown him years earlier and set up camp. He lived as a hermit. Drove over the mountain to Idaho Springs every few weeks for supplies. His hair grew long and tangled with bits of leaves, a twig. He ate without interest and hiked endlessly so that he became gaunt in the face and lean-muscled about the calves and thighs. Occasionally, hikers chanced upon him on the mountain trails, and they would back away in caution, step off the trail, and give him wide berth.

All summer, he watched from above as the crews blasted rock into the diversion tunnels, sealing them, allowing the river to reclaim its ancestral course until it flowed into the concrete block of the dam and began backing up. The water rose in the valley, filling in depressions, swallowing up familiar landmarks. A stock tank a half mile out appeared to slowly sink into the reservoir; a grove of willow brush by the old riverbank disappeared overnight. He sat on his haunches one morning drinking coffee, watching as the first tentative fingers of water groped at the outskirts of town then flowed down Main Street and spread into side roads and alleys. Before many more days, the water lapped at the burned-out mounds of the demolished buildings, and by July, only the blackened outlines of the rubbish heaps were visible, like small volcanic islands poking from the ocean.

Once, when Clayton was a teenager fishing out near

the mouth of the Chesapeake, he came upon a pod of manta rays hovering on the surface, oval-winged bodies absorbing the heat of the sun. Looking down at the shadows of what once was the town, he thought back to those rays and again felt the draw of the sea.

By late August, much of the low-lying terrain lay under a film of water rusted from the sediment. Most of the construction activity had ended, and crew camps were thinning out. Then one day, Clayton saw a long line of flatbed trucks filing up the highway from Denver. They made their way to a section of high ground just outside the old town limits and idled beside a backhoe. The backhoe spat a cloud of black smoke from its exhaust, and then the bucket lowered and began gouging the earth. Once a sizable hole had been dug, two men climbed into it, each carrying what looked like a length of canvas strap. After several minutes, they climbed back out and attached the straps with hooks to the bucket of the backhoe. Slowly, the operator raised the bucket until the straps tightened and seemed to strain against some great weight, and from the hole emerged a casket cradled in the straps. The men guided the casket onto the first flatbed, then the backhoe and the truck crept forward a few feet and the backhoe again violated the earth. Clayton watched all day. They disinterred three graves per hour. Each flatbed held eight caskets. By the end of the second day, twelve trucks were loaded with the last residents of town, and the convoy turned east and disappeared back from where they came. The scarred cemetery lay empty, pockmarked, awaiting the water.

Clayton spent one more night on the mountain, completely alone now. He woke early and boiled coffee on the coals and ate a piece of bread and looked out over the valley. He watched the morning light glance off the water. He picked up a fistful of dirt and let it sift through his clenched hand. He dug into the ground and pinched a bit of earth and tasted it. He remembered back to the farm, when his father would sample the soil each spring and was able to judge what fertilizer was needed for the season, what amendments. He could judge which crops would thrive in each section just by taking a bit of soil on his tongue and letting his saliva mix with it and then spitting it out. Clayton could himself taste life in the earth: metallic, woody, a hint of salt. He looked down at the water. *This was life*, he thought, *the earth at my feet, the water below.* Always the water, calling, calling. What life could he feel inside himself now? No warmth to the blood, no force. He had hibernated these years. Lost. Not living at all. The choice? *Will I make a choice sometime in my life*, he asked himself. *Once? It is time*, he acknowledged to himself that morning. *Nora was right: it is time.*

He drove down the mountain into Denver. The bustle

and traffic unnerved him, but he took a room at a motel on the outskirts of town. He showered and shaved his beard and visited a barbershop. Then he found a phone booth and called Sonny.

"Where you been, boy? Been trying to contact you for a week."

Clayton almost did not recognize his voice because it didn't have the usual lightness to it. "I spent some time in the hills. Camping, thinking."

"I got news, Clayton."

"I'm listening."

"You got anybody close?"

"Just tell me."

"Your dad."

Clayton paused. He took in a great breath. From the phone booth, he caught sight of a boy walking across the street, looking nervously in one direction then the other. *Late for a boy to be out alone*, Clayton thought, and he was suddenly panicked for him, terrified. A boy's life, cars, a delicate balance. Clayton held that breath until the boy had run across the street. Then he exhaled. "What about my dad?"

"He's passed, Clayton. Found him in the woods. I'm saddened to tell you. I wish I could tell you more. Where he was when they found him, the details. I just don't know."

"I know where they found him." Clayton drifted

back to Virginia in his mind, the grassy hill in the woods, the hallowed embankment. He pictured his father there, another casualty of war. "I know exactly where they found him. I just don't know why. I thought he sounded better last I talked to him."

"Don't question the why," Sonny said. "They had bills. I guess your father figured the veterans' benefit would cover the debt, let them keep the house."

"Jesus," Clayton said. "I should've known. I'm headed back."

"That's good. But your mother, she's not herself."

"I can help maybe."

"No. Right now, she don't want nothing to do with you. Sorry to be so forward. She'll get over it. Give her time."

five

Sand Point had changed during Clayton's years away. He almost missed the turnoff from the state highway because a strip mall now occupied what had been soybean fields. The winding road to Sand Point still followed the same curves and dips as before, but now it was made of macadam rather than dirt and crushed shell. As he neared the beach, tourist shops popped up along the road, little boutiques displaying sleek bathing suits and cover-ups, knickknack stores hawking T-shirts, beach chairs, conch shells not found within six hundred miles of these shores.

He had driven past his mother's house in Richmond on his way east. He had not stopped. He would at some point. He owed her, and he felt like he owed himself. A reconnection, a family. But he did not know how to approach her. He felt so guilty. He had asked Sonny by phone, but Sonny had said, "Come on back, we'll talk it out, figure a plan," and Clayton had trusted his word. Sonny would help mend the wounds that separated Clayton from his mother. But for now, his concern was with Sand Point, what remained there for him to resolve. It looked so foreign to him now.

And then he passed Walter Pine's fish market. It remained part of the past—the same dirt parking lot, the same austere cinder-block structure—except now it was painted robin's-egg blue with a red tin roof that reminded Clayton of pictures he had seen of Caribbean villages. He did not slow his truck, but his grip tightened on the wheel and his head pivoted involuntarily to keep the market in view until the trees obscured his sight line. The market was the reason he had returned, but he could not will himself to pull into the parking lot to find out who might still be there, who might be long gone.

Clayton drove on into town and stopped at a grocery

store near the beach that stocked supplies for the tourists who rented beach houses during the summer. Only a few days remained in August, and the season was winding to a close, tanning oils and beach towels marked half price. He collected some canned goods, a six-pack, a loaf of bread. An older man worked the checkout line, but Clayton did not recognize him from earlier days.

"Things slowing down for you some." It was more of a comment from Clayton than a question.

The old man nodded. "Still get the weekend trade until the weather turns."

"Been a while since I was here last. Place has grown up a bit."

"Turn around and someone's putting up another cottage. Damn fools building right over the dune. Storm will knock them all into the sea."

"Looks like there's still some open beach down south." Clayton felt a constriction in his throat, his voice sounding hoarse. Other than his short conversation with Sonny, he realized he had not spoken more than a few words aloud in more than four months.

"State's protecting it. Set it aside. Won't allow development. It's the last piece of open sand between here and the state line."

Clayton helped the man bag the rest of his groceries. "I noticed the old fish market's still open. The Pines still run it?" He tried to sound casual, wondered if the tension in his chest revealed itself in his voice.

"Oh, yeah. Well, just the missus since the old man passed."

"Passed?" Clayton again affected an air, inquisitive, like he was unaware of the news. He just needed to hear it from someone other than Sonny.

"A while back."

"How far back?"

"Oh, a good while ago. Stroke or some such."

"It hasn't changed much, except for the paint."

"No. The tourists wouldn't want it to. It's what they expect. What they call 'quaint.' An institution around here."

Another customer lined up at the counter, and Clayton knew the man's attention was turning to his work. But he had come this far, he had to finish, so he bought some time by fumbling in his pocket for correct change. "So, his wife still run the market? Loretta, was that her name?"

"Yes."

"I suppose she's remarried?"

"Loretta, a sweet lady. Has attracted her share of attention since the old man passed. I don't recall if she's taken another husband yet."

Clayton drove to the south end of the beach. Clouds were building to the east, so he grabbed his poncho and walked in the direction of the state preserve. On the path to the shore, he passed through a stand of scrub oak that held an assortment of songbirds flitting between the thick growths and scolding his encroachment. He reached the dune, where tufts of sea oats grew in tight bunches that fluttered in the breeze. From the crest, he paused to take in the sweep of the deserted beach and the ocean beyond, and then he walked the high tide mark for two miles with only the gulls for company. His mind played back the information he had learned from the grocer, but he could not decide what to do. He had lived without hope for so long that now he was afraid to let it seep back into his assessment of life's possibilities. A part of him believed that it was enough to know that she was safe now, removed from harm's way, doing well.

A squall was building out in the Atlantic. Sky and sea merged blue-gray, and the offshore storm showed a lighter curtain of rain against the darker sky. From a distance, it appeared as if the clouds were drawing water up from the sea into them. Rain moved closer, the wind stiffening, lightning dancing on the horizon. Clayton burrowed into a dune, hooded himself with the poncho, and watched the squall pass overhead in a swift, drenching, thunder-cracking charge. Afterward, the ionized air smelled new and salty. The water grew oil-slick calm and reflected an almost iridescent green. Far out, a few shafts of sunlight broke from the clouds and painted a line of ocean cream-yellow. Clayton rose from the dune feeling almost reborn and walked back to his truck to reunite with Sonny and see about his boats and gear. He was grateful Sonny had not sold them off.

▶ ▶ ▶

Clayton guided his johnboat along the tidal creek. The marshland spreading out from the main channel had saved this section of bay from development, and it remained much as he had left it a decade earlier. His crab pots, which Sonny had stored with care under a plastic tarp behind the garage, were also of that past age, so as he motored out to check his buoy line, time was suspended for a moment and he could enjoy the freedom of being alone in a boat on the water. He harvested his crabs, neither as numerous as before nor as large, but still there. Whatever changed above the surface, as long as the blue crab still scuttled below, something vital and worthwhile remained of this place. This is what he had wanted all along: to be on the water. Squint-eyed, brown-skinned, baked by the sun—to be alive on the water.

When he pulled alongside Walter's old dock, he wandered back in time. How often had he moored at this dock, hoping for a glimpse from Loretta? What right had he to ask back into her life, so many years lost? Would she even recognize him? Time reshapes memory. Had she actually cared for him as he for her? Was loathing reflected in her eyes during that last horrible meeting between them? He unloaded his basket of crabs and moved heavily toward the store, feeling as awkward as a teenager. It was still early, no traffic on the road, the market not yet open. Time enough for him to reconsider. Except, as he passed the back living quarters, she was standing in the window looking out at him. His breath caught. He stopped there, holding his crabs like an offering. Loretta stood motionless behind the window. There was nothing in her expression that gave him hope. She was passive, like marble. She had matured into a sorrowful beauty. It was heartbreaking for Clayton to take in. She looked older than her years, yet timeless, her life reflected in her eyes. Finally, she turned from the window and was gone.

Clayton continued around to the front of the market. The door was closed. He tested the knob: locked. He lowered his basket and sat on the front step and stared into the dirt. He sat there, thinking his own thoughts: remorse, regret, despair. He grew weary with the weight of his burden. He slumped forward, elbows on knees, and prayed. He did not know how, he had not had practice, but he concentrated on the times he had tried to do right in his life, to connect with the forlorn Loretta, to will his father to health, to give comfort to Nora, and, in time, he eased into a kind of meditative trance. And his prayer floated in the humid southern air and condensed into an image of his life. Although barely into his third decade, he realized the regret-filled visions of an old man—they saw what might have been. A life lived one way rather than another, choices made and, worse, not made. But he was back on the water now, reborn, and he gave thanks for that. He felt the sun on his face, smelled the sea on the breeze, and heard the crabs scratching in his crate. He looked down at his hands, nicked by the wire of the traps and the sharp points of shell. A waterman's hands. He dozed, content in his resolve.

He thought he heard—dreamt—footsteps on the floorboards, a key working a lock, a door creaking open. He woke to the touch of a hand caressing his cheek.

Migration

Herding Instinct

Patterns

One morning during the summer of his sixteenth year, 1962, Jeffrey looked up from his chores as his father, Enid Pugh, emerged from the house cradling a lever-action .30-30 in the crook of his right arm. He walked to where Jeffrey was shoveling manure and wasted hay from around the feeding racks beside the barn. The day was raw for early June—a sharp wind was blowing from the northwest, low clouds were spitting sleet onto newly green fields. Jeffrey wore leather gloves and a canvas jacket with the collar pulled close against his neck but still felt the weather's sting. Manure steamed in the wheelbarrow he filled.

"Them's ninety-seven head there," Enid said when Jeffery set aside his shovel and came to him. He swung the barrel of the rifle in the general direction of the sheep grazing in the near pasture. "Sixty-three ewes, thirty-four ewe lambs. You need to push them on up to the summer range. When you come down in August, I expect to count

▶

175

sixty-three ewes, thirty-four ewe lambs."

"Me and Russell?" Jeffrey asked.

"I didn't say that, did I?"

"No, sir. It's just that … "

"I hauled the camp trailer up last week. Take this here weapon. And one of the dogs. Don't matter which. Leave after breakfast; should be there before dark."

Jeffrey nodded and went to the barn and stripped off his rubber boots that had accumulated the muck from the sheep pens. He tilted back his work cap, a sweat-stained green John Deere, and looked off to the east. Behind the cover of clouds, he knew snow still clung to the peaks and in the shadows of the pines. But the high meadows were clearing and beginning to grow thick with grass.

The ranch and its livestock fenced the whole of Jeffrey's world, so the responsibility of minding the smaller of his father's two flocks would not normally have concerned him. The ways of sheep were as much a part of his being as the red was to the mesas rising from the valley to the southwest. And, unlike his sheep, Jeffrey had always been a loner, never felt the need for companionship. He was content to pass the days on the small family ranch taking care of chores and wandering the surrounding hills. "Born to the rancher's life," his mother said. So, summer-range duty—searching for strays, tending the sick, and watch-ing for the occasional coyote—should have excited him.

Especially now, as Russell apparently would not be with him. But this summer, it did not. This summer, he had had other plans.

Until early the past spring, Jeffrey had never felt quite at ease in school. He invariably took the last desk in the last row in every class. Because he was sturdy for his age, tall and filled out and handsome in a roughly hewn manner, his classmates accepted Jeffrey with a cautious friendliness, including him in invitations to parties, school dances, movies. He rarely accepted. A certain shyness that some adults would label as dullness of mind directed his actions.

But recently, he had begun to feel more comfortable with the other boys as they matured and as their voices deepened to match his own. They no longer appeared as breakable as they once had when they wrestled in the schoolyard. And the girls had taken on a softness and shapeliness that aroused in Jeffrey a desire to remain near to them, within eyesight, within touching distance.

On the first warm weekend in May, Katherine Ann, a town girl whose father ran the insurance office, had invited a group of friends to the movies and to her house afterward for a cookout. Jeffrey had dressed in a starched white shirt with mother-of-pearl snap buttons and his newest jeans. During the movie, Katherine Ann sat beside him, and while the other girls twittered over Elvis in western costume, she had slipped her arm through Jeffrey's and whispered to him that Elvis did not look much like a cowboy to her, that she bet he could ride circles around him. Later that night, in the darkness of Katherine Ann's backyard, she had teased him about his shyness, pressed the full length of her body against his, and kissed him with experience that caused Jeffrey's knees to buckle.

His outlook on life shifted dramatically that evening. His vision of the future turned away from the lonesome, sheep-studded pastures and toward flashing jukeboxes, tight sweaters, and soft hands uncalloused by outdoor work. Yes, this summer was supposed to be different.

Jeffrey walked back from the barn to the house as if he were still bogged in the muck of the sheep pens.

In the kitchen, Jeffrey's mother was setting a large dish of scrambled eggs on the table beside an equally large bowl of fried potatoes, a platter of ham, and a stack of toast. Lucille Pugh was a woman who seemed too small for ranch life. She appeared shrunk into herself, with eyes downcast and head bowed ever so slightly, as if she were about to offer an apology or a prayer.

Enid scooped half the eggs onto his plate and passed the dish to Jeffrey, who took a small spoonful and, in turn, passed it on to his mother.

"Take your fill," Lucille said to Jeffrey, pushing the bowl back his way. "I probably didn't make enough. I can fix more."

"I got more than plenty," Jeffrey said, adding a ham steak to his plate.

As he reached for the toast, he heard the rumbling of a motorcycle outside and, looking across the table, noticed for the first time that there was no plate set for his brother. After a few seconds, the kitchen door flew open and Russell stomped in, blowing on his hands.

"Colder than a well-digger's ass on that bike," he said, walking to his mother and planting a quick kiss on the top of her head. "Just in time for grub, I see." He turned to his seat, then stared at the bare setting.

Lucille began to slide back her chair, but Enid shot her a look that stopped her short.

Russell glared at his father. "What, you expect me to eat from the bowls?"

Enid bent back over his plate and began scooping potatoes into his mouth. When he answered, food spit from his lips. "You gone out of here yesterday afternoon, all night, half today, and you expect to be fed when you wander back?"

"I had business in town last night."

"I hope your business included a big meal, because I'll be goddammed if you're getting anything here. Not until you earn it."

"Earn it? Earn it? I haven't set foot off this place for

two solid weeks. If it wasn't for you using young Jeff and me for slave labor, you would've lost this place years ago."

Russell advanced a step toward Enid, who gripped his table knife and raised it as he half stood from his chair. Lucille gasped. Russell spun on his heels and stormed out the door. Lucille began to rise.

"Sit down and finish your breakfast," Enid said.

"My appetite is gone."

"Sit down. There'll be no waste at this table. Eat."

After finishing his meal and packing a small duffel bag, Jeffrey went to the barn to collect some gear. He whistled for Scottie, the oldest of their border collies, slow but dependable. Russell was working on his motorcycle by the lambing pen. He had disassembled the carburetor and had the parts soaking in a pan of gasoline.

"How you doing, little brother?"

"He's sending me up to graze the sheep."

"Got the graveyard duty, huh? Tough luck."

Jeffrey had spent the last two summers with Russell on the upper meadows before Russell had rebelled last year when he turned twenty. He had given his father an ultimatum: find someone else to shepherd or he would leave. His father needed the help.

"Son of a bitch is too cheap to hire out one of the Basques, or even a Chilean. They don't hardly charge a cent."

Jeffrey loved his older brother, even idolized him. But he did not understand him at all. Russell had no allegiance to the land or to the livestock, and for the past few years, he had been counting the days until he could save enough from part-time town work to be rid of the place for good. Jeffrey could not imagine life removed from the ranch, the freedom of the open spaces and wide views. Until recently, until Katherine Ann, he had seen little to recommend itself to city life.

Jeffrey retrieved a can of disinfectant from the medicine shelf and packed it in his bag. "I'm not real excited about this job," he told Russell. "To tell the honest truth, I had other things in mind this summer. I met this girl."

"Why, you young buck," Russell teased. "You finally discovered what the finer things in life are all about."

Jeffrey looked at his brother out of the corner of his eye. "Not home last night. You find action?"

"That, my little brother, is none of your business. Your ears are too innocent to take it all in." Russell reached for a five-eighths-inch wrench and pointed it at Jeffrey. "But tell you what. If you're real nice to me, lick my boots and all, I might just spell you every once in a while this summer. On one of my slow nights, when the old crank needs a rest, you know what I mean?"

Jeffrey said, "Right," and headed out the door.

He loved these rare moments when his brother actually treated him something like an equal rather than a little boy. More often, Russell ignored him altogether, almost as if he had lumped Jeffrey into that big rubbish pile of things soon to be dumped: the ranch, his father, Jeffrey.

Outside, Jeffrey led Scottie, who had heeled at his whistle, toward the sheep. A black-and-white mix, the border collie's washed-out coat and rheumy eyes showed his age, but his step livened as he ran into the field. Jeffrey positioned the dog at the back of the flock, culled a few head nearest him, and began herding them to the main gate, shooing them from behind, as if they were a gaggle of geese. With Scottie's yapping, the body of the flock ambled after the lead group. Passing the house, a white clapboard in need of the brush, Jeffrey saw his mother framed in the kitchen window and raised his hand in a half wave.

Enid held open the gate. "Watch for bloat from the new grass. Keep them from that clover on the south end."

The summer meadows were eight miles from the ranch. Jeffrey followed the fence line past the barn and up the county road for three miles. Just beyond Soda Creek, swollen by spring runoff into an angry boil, he turned the flock onto a logging track that climbed through boulder-studded aspen groves to the summit of the rise. From there, the road dropped between a notch in the hills and onto the green open range of the high country. Because his father held the grazing rights from the Bureau of Land

Management, the field was clear of other livestock. Empty, it waited for Jeffrey and his sheep.

The weather had lifted some since morning. The sun pushed through breaks in the clouds, warming the afternoon and bathing the distant meadow in long swaths of light that shifted over the land and made it a living thing, like a great flat animal arching its back to the warmth. At the near end of the meadow, Jeffrey saw the camp trailer beside a stream lined with stunted aspen. The grasslands were enclosed on three sides by spruce forest that climbed the sides of the mountains and on the fourth side by a talus slope that angled for several hundred feet before leveling into another meadow far below.

Jeffrey bedded the sheep on the streamside closest to the trailer so he could check their hooves for gravel or cactus thorns picked up along the trail. By the time he finished a cursory inspection, dark twilight had settled over the valley. As the shadows crept across the fields, Jeffrey's mood darkened with the skies. Shoulders stooped from weariness, he slumped against the wheel of the camp wagon and thought of the pressure of Katherine Ann's body against his, the soft give of her lips, and he cursed his father. When he absently picked a blade of grass and held it between his teeth, he tasted her sweetness, and he cursed the sheep.

Jeffrey jerked awake from his dream when Scottie

nuzzled his leg, begging dinner. He shook off his drowsi-ness and climbed into the cramped trailer and searched for the cooking stove. From the provision box, he took a tin of corned beef and a can of beans. Back outside, he lit the stove, scooped half the beef and all of the beans into a skillet, and dumped the rest of the beef into Scottie's metal feed dish. When the food had warmed, he ate from the skillet and watched night come. The sheep were bedding down in a tightly huddled scrum of fleece. The dog curled at his feet. Jeffrey realized he had not spoken a word aloud since he and his brother had talked earlier that morning.

▶ ▶ ▶

The first few days at the summer range gave Jeffrey little time to brood as he arranged the camp according to his needs. The shepherd's wagon was of simple homemade construction: a two-wheeled flatbed barely eight feet long with slatted wood sides and a metal roof. Inside, a plank extended the full length and half the width of the trailer to hold a sleeping mat. The other side was fitted with narrow shelves for storage. Jeffrey placed the medicines and treat-ments on the first shelf just inside the trailer door, within easy reach but protected from the weather. He stowed away a change of clothes and the rifle and ammunition under his sleeping shelf. Near the creek, he fashioned a crude pen of aspen saplings to isolate any animals that fell ill. Two sheep quickly developed bloat from overgrazing the pasture's new growth and had to be treated with baking soda and warm water. Another bloated so severely that Jeffrey had to force a plastic tube down her throat into her rumen to ease her discomfort.

Jeffrey had worried about bearing sole responsibility for the flock without Russell's guidance, but the daily routine instilled in him a growing confidence. He loved being alone in the mountains, working close to the land, close to the weather, as part of every squall that blew up over the peaks. And he loved walking with Scottie among the sheep that so depended on him for their welfare. As he thought about it, Russell had not been an active partner in their range duty during the past two summers anyway. He had been forever running off into town, leaving Jeffrey alone to make due as best he could.

But even when days were filled with activity, the slow draw of evening followed. When the world beyond his campfire grew dark and dense as a granite wall and the sky overhead blossomed with pinpoints of light in numbers too great to comprehend, Jeffrey gazed into the burning tinder of his campfire and saw Katherine Ann. Her image faded and grew, dancing in the flickering curl of the flame. As the nights passed, one into another, his emotions would alternate between an almost painful aching for Katherine Ann and a growing irritation with his older brother for his hollow promise to give Jeffrey the occasional break from shepherding.

The days began taking on a sameness that flowed together. Jeffrey rose before the sun, checked his flock, steeped and drank coffee, and heated beans or soup that he ate with hard biscuits. After breakfast, he left Scottie with the sheep and hiked into the cool, quiet shadows of the forest. He practiced his marksmanship on pinecones and often stalked game for the thrill of the hunt, even though he never shot anything larger than the occasional fox squirrel or rabbit to add to the cooking pot. His tracking skills were finely tuned, almost a sixth sense, developed from sixteen years spent on the land, in the fields, every day. He tracked animals without even thinking about it, the way a heart beats unconsciously in a chest. He would catch sight of a chipmunk scampering over a rock and before he realized what he was doing, he would be holding it in his hand. He once plucked a green-throated hummingbird from the air as it hovered over a patch of columbines.

Jeffrey never traveled so far from the flock that he could not catch sight of them from the edge of the forest, and he was able to tell almost instinctively if they required his attention. One afternoon during his fourth week on the range, he sensed a general nervousness among his sheep. Scottie was working more actively than usual, scrambling with his muzzle close to the ground, herding one ewe, then another that had broken from the main band. The Rambouillet mixes they bred possessed dependable herding instincts, so any attempt to scatter was cause for alarm. Jeffrey set off across the pasture in a steady jog. By the time he had reached the stream, he could hear the high whine of a motorcycle winding down the gravel road. Russell pulled into the field, eased up beside Jeffrey, and cut the engine.

"Hey, little brother. Your friends seem a little jumpy." Russell nodded toward the sheep.

"I believe they have forgot the sound of your bike. It's pretty quiet up here."

"Don't I know it. Like the inside of a coffin." Russell reached around for a bulging saddlebag and tossed it to Jeffrey. "A little restock on your grub. And some home cooking from Mom."

"No need for you to truck this up here. Still got a near-full provision box."

"My pleasure, believe me. The old man has run me about to the limit. Besides," he continued, "the old bastard was worried about his stock. Wanted to make sure you hadn't run them over the cliff." Russell looked over at the sheep dismissively. "Dumb shits is worthless, if you ask me. Bring in just enough to keep you in debt to the bankers."

Jeffrey began unpacking the saddlebag. "Give me a minute, and I'll cook us up something."

"Don't bother. I got to be pushing on. I escaped that prison, and I ain't about to go back until I take a turn in town."

Jeffrey scuffed his boot in the grass and tossed the empty bag back to Russell.

Town. He wanted badly to remind his brother of his promise, but he could not speak. So long alone, the words would not come. Russell kick-started the motorcycle, revved it, then let it idle while his eyes seemed to wander across the rolling fields, into the blue forest beyond.

"Tell you what," Russell said without looking at his brother. "Why don't you plan on washing out a clean shirt by next Friday. I'll spell you up here. You can take the bike."

"That would suit me fine," Jeffrey said. He felt like high stepping over to his brother and wrapping him in a bear hug. Instead, he pulled his cap down low over his eyes and stared at the ground. "Thanks."

▶ ▶ ▶

During the next week, summer settled into the valley. Almost overnight, Indian paintbrush and mountain asters sprang up along the creek bank and the yellow-green aspen leaves deepened in color, took on density. The morning sky reflected a rock-solid blue before giving way to great billowing clouds in the afternoon. The pace of Jeffrey's life slowed with the tempo of the season. He spent one entire afternoon on his back in the meadow watching the cloud formations scud by.

When Russell showed up on Friday evening, Jeffery allowed his excitement to surface. He had been reigning himself in all week in the event his brother would forget him. But when he saw Russell bouncing down the logging track, he quickly changed into the shirt and jeans he had set out just in case.

On the motorcycle ride into town, he stopped twice to comb down his wind-tangled hair, and as he pulled in front of Katherine Ann's house, he paused before pushing the bell to rub his teeth with his left index finger.

Katherine Ann answered his ring dressed in a black-striped halter top and hip-huggers. The hallway light shone through her hair so that she seemed an apparition, softer that flesh, lighter than air. "Hey, Jeff. What are you doing here?"

"Just stopped by, thought we might catch a movie." He caught sight of a small group of people in the living room, all townies, he believed. The boys wore pressed Bermuda shorts and madras shirts and leather sandals. He blushed at his blue jeans and flannel.

"Gee, I'm busy tonight. Why didn't you call?"

"I've been away. I'm away most of the time ... I just thought—"

"Listen, Jeff, I've got to run. Maybe some other time. Give me a call."

Later that night, Jeffrey watched the party from the shadows of a juniper hedge, the boys showing off by doing handstands on the back lawn, the girls tossing their hair and flirting with quick birdlike movements. Near midnight, he saw a boy he recognized as a senior linebacker and a clumsy horseman lead Katherine Ann behind a spruce tree not a dozen feet away where he then kissed her neck and ran his hands over her arching body. Jeffrey lurked in the shadows as the party ended, as the house lights darkened, then he rode without purpose for hours, arriving back at the camp just after sunrise.

Russell sat by the stove drinking coffee. Jeffrey dismounted and tossed his brother the keys.

"Have fun?" Russell asked.

"It was fine."

"Not going to let your big brother in on the dirty details?"

"Nothing much to tell. Just a movie and all."

"Forget the movie. I'm just interested in the 'and all' stuff."

"Nothing much."

"Till daybreak?"

"I rode some. Filled your tank though."

Russell straddled his bike with his feet spread wide

on the ground and studied Jeffrey. "Give me a couple of weeks and I'll babysit for you again."

"No need."

"I don't mind."

"Really. No need. I'm fine up here."

"Suit yourself, but sometimes you act as crazy as those sheep."

Russell revved the engine, shifted into gear, and disappeared up the road, into the trees.

Jeffrey drank the coffee Russell had made and finished off some potatoes left in the skillet. He thought about sleeping. His legs were heavy and his head felt detached from his body, floating just above his shoulders. But he knew he would not be able to rest, so he hiked along the stream bank until he spotted some fresh tracks in the wet earth, and then he was off in his own world again, moving with purpose, crouched close to the ground, following his prey. Lost in the hunt, he forgot Katherine Ann, forgot Russell, forgot his father, forgot everything and everyone beyond the meadow and the surrounding forest. For a while at least.

Monday afternoon, Enid showed up at the camp. After driving the rump-sprung old Ford along the rutted track, he was in no mood for idle conversation.

"You seen Russell?" he asked Jeffrey without saying hello.

"Not lately," Jeffrey answered, neither lying nor being completely truthful. "Why?"

"I run him off. He up and left Friday after lunch with us, right in the middle of fencing. Come back dragging ass Saturday morning, and I told him to clear the hell out. Sick of his whoring and drinking. Told him to stay away until he could pull his weight around the ranch like a growed man. Thought he might've run up here."

"I ain't seen him."

"He shows himself, I don't want you feeding him, I don't want you giving him drink, I don't want you lending him a pot to piss in. Understand?"

"I understand."

"See how long he can last on his own without the free handouts I been giving him these past twenty years." Enid still had not climbed down from his truck. The exhaust from the running engine fouled the clean mountain air. He looked out over his flock in the far pasture. "That'un alone over there looks to be favoring her left foreleg. May need to trim her hooves."

"Yes, sir."

Enid shifted the truck into reverse and wheeled it around for his return trip without saying another word. Jeffrey watched the dust rise from the road and watched it settle back down, and he did not know whether to feel guilty for contributing to his brother's exile or envious of

▶ Gary Schanbacher

192

him for being rid of their father.

▸ ▸ ▸

By early August, Jeffrey no longer missed the company of other people, and he fought off dreams of Katherine Ann whenever he could. Company meant little when you had nothing to say to begin with, and as far as Katherine Ann was concerned, well, there was no sense dreaming about someone so completely out of reach. He had been a fool to think himself at her level. He was best off in the high country and alone on the ranch, away from all those opportunities to fail. Besides, he loved the outdoor work and all that came with it: the midday summer sun that burned through the thin air, the winter blizzards that buried fence lines and brought on cold that froze birds in flight. Sometimes during a heavy rain, he would wander out into the meadow, let the rain beat down on him, and feel himself melting into the earth. His father had always cursed the hard life, and it had beaten him, turned him against any warm feeling. But Jeffrey accepted what nature threw at him as part of what it meant to be alive, here, now, and he knew he could succeed in this place that had beat down his father and his brother.

As the nights began taking on a chill, Jeffrey fretted about his return to civilization and to school. The prospect of his junior year in high school no longer excited him. His days became filled with minor irritations: the same old beans and beef; the utter stupidity of the sheep, who were forever spooking at their shadow or wandering too close to the steep slope at the edge of the meadow; the dog too slow to respond to his whistled commands. His sleep became restless, and that restlessness may have saved his flock from the pack of dogs.

They came howling up the valley early in the morning, just before the full moon in August. From somewhere in that fitful sleep, tracing the edge of his consciousness, Jeffrey heard their baying off in the distance, so far away it seemed a part of his dream. Then came Scottie's warning yips, and Jeffrey was up and out the door in an instant, firmly gripping the forestock of his rifle, running toward the flock.

The dogs had not yet crested the lower hill to his upper pasture, but he could hear them now, barking as they ran, probably picking up the scent of his sheep. Coyotes were a danger to the flock, but they were shy animals that feared the smell of humans and came for the sheep only when lambs were available for easy culling or when their natural prey grew scarce. But pack dogs, ranch dogs run wild, did not fear man. They scattered flocks for sport, ripping and tearing through the ranks.

Jeffrey positioned himself between the flock and the crest of the hill just as the first dog came loping into view from below. In the dim light, it appeared to be a collie. Behind it followed two hounds, a pure shepherd, and two of mixed breed. Jeffery shot the lead dog head on, just below the neck. It dropped, instantly dead. The other dogs seemed confused and slowed in their advance toward the sheep. He took one hound broadside through the shoulders as it turned to sniff at the lead dog. The remaining four howled then scattered and broke back down the hill. Jeffrey could have left it at that; the dogs were on the run. But he was suddenly filled with anger—two months of watching over his flock day and night without a loss could have been ruined in one unlucky night. He shot all the dogs as they fled. The last, the shepherd, he took from one-hundred-fifty yards out on a dead run away from him. His bullet must have caught its spine because it cartwheeled once, kicked its forelegs wildly, and attempted to drag its hindquarters several staggering yards before it settled into a curl and grew still.

Scottie had held the sheep in a tight bunch during the shooting, and Jeffrey found no injuries among them. If allowed to run when spooked, they might break a leg or die from exhaustion or heart attack. Enid had turned a few bucks in with the flock in late July, and many newly pregnant ewes surely would have aborted if they had been run hard. Scottie had done his job, and Jeffrey rewarded him with extra rations.

> ▶ ▶ ▶

During the waning days of summer, the sheep prospered under Jeffrey's watch and Scottie's vigilance, growing fat on the mountain grass. But frost on the pasture signaled that summer grazing was coming to an end.

By late August, the air carried a dusky, wood-burnt scent and the afternoon sun cast long shadows across the meadow. At sundown, Jeffrey listened to the keening of bull elk from the black edge of the forest as they began to assemble their harems for mating. The high, soulful bugle triggered a yearning in Jeffrey, as it must have in the cow elks, and he began to stir for companionship. His success at keeping the flock together and whole during the summer renewed in him the confidence that perhaps he could succeed in the world of people also, that perhaps if he set his mind to it, he could find the same sense of accomplishment in the lower world as he had in the higher. The last days of camp before he would drive the flock back down to the ranch for wintering were spent in hopeful anticipation. His dreams of Katherine Ann, or rather of a girl like Katherine Ann, returned.

It was during one of those dreams that the sharp buzzing of a chain saw jarred him awake and caused him to bolt upright from his mat. In the foggy seconds it took his head to clear, the chain saw became a motor-cycle, a motorcycle so close it seemed to roar just outside his trailer. For the second time in less than two weeks, Jeffrey took up the rifle and ran to his sheep. There in the meadow, illuminated by the full moon as if he were caught in a spotlight, Russell was charging through the flock, whooping and hollering, causing panic. A girl sat behind him, her arms wrapped tightly around his waist. Jeffrey counted four ewes down and appearing lifeless. Another two were limping horribly, and the entire band was being stampeded toward the steep shelf at the far end of the pasture.

For a second, Jeffrey's world went dark and his father's warning pounded in his head—*in August, I expect to count sixty-three ewes, thirty-four ewe lambs.*

When he regained his senses, Jeffrey was looking down the barrel of his .30-30. The sighting bead rested just above the girl's head in the center of Russell's back. Jeffrey cradled the stock of the rifle against his right cheek and held the bead between Russell's shoulder blades for a long moment and felt the pressure of the trigger in the first finger of his right hand. Ever so slightly, the pressure increased, the sighting bead held steady. The noise of the motorcycle died away, the bleating of the sheep, Scottie's barking—all silent, the night absolutely still. The motorcycle ceased moving, frozen in time. No motion, no sound, no existence other than Jeffrey and his brother, bonded together by a bridge of hollow steel.

Then, almost as if with no conscious decision of his own, his finger relaxed on the trigger and he lowered the gun from his shoulder. The world picked up speed again, resumed spinning on its axis. Jeffrey watched his brother race through the sheep, scattering them every which way, while Scottie ran in ever widening circles attempting to gather the flock. Setting his rifle in the grass beside the banked fire, Jeffrey crawled into the trailer and stuffed his duffel bag with clothes and several tins of food. He climbed back out and looked toward his brother, who was now bouncing his motorcycle across the field, waving his hat in one hand, half standing on the footrests. The girl sat cross-legged in the center of the meadow. The sheep looked like whitecaps scattered across an angry, dark sea. Jeffrey turned and began hiking up the dirt road that would take him past his family's ranch before daylight and out onto the state highway by morning and from there to wherever the truckers might carry him.

Laws of Gravity

During our wedding, a wildfire broke out in the meadow above the mountain chapel, raising a curtain of smoke that veiled the sun. When a light shower of ash began floating down on us like black snowflakes, the small gathering retreated from the flower garden into the church. All except Shelly and me and the markedly unenthusiastic minister. Shelly twirled slowly about the blooming clusters of columbines and Rocky Mountain iris, her arms raised to heaven, an occasional fleck of ash smudging her cheek or alighting on her gown.

We abandoned the garden only when the scream of fire trucks drowned out our vows. I should have known right then and there: I should have known our marriage was destined to suffer more than its share of fire and smoke; I should have guessed the sun would always remain partially obscured.

Really, our wedding went well, all things considered.

▶

The guests maintained a reasonable degree of sobriety until after the ceremony. No one protested the nondenominational service, though several outspoken atheists attended as well as an assortment of Buddhists, Hare Krishna, sorcerers, and at least one Druid. And Shelly had indulged my desire for a traditional service. As a second-year law student, my naive concern for legal sanction and my devotion to the sanctity of jurisprudence was certainly as finely honed then as it would ever be during my ensuing career. So, at a time when fashion dictated the crafting of highly personalized, breast-baring wedding vows, ours were straight from the Book of Common Prayer, with one exception: Shelly refused to include the passage "until we are parted by death." She had no issue with "in sickness and in health," or even with "honor and keep him," but flatly rejected the promise of a union unto death.

"You are mine and I am yours right now, this second," she explained to me in front of the entire congregation. "But forever? Come on, who's to say? I could age into a spiteful old hag. You could grow fat and lazy and hateful. Let's just concentrate on today. Let the tomorrows take care of themselves."

How could I argue? The wildfire had already disrupted the service, and I had no desire to prolong it further by debating the expediency of deviating from the prescribed liturgy. Besides, I could tell that the audience was growing restless: the hum of softly chanted mantras drifted from the rear of the chapel; my advisor from law school, a doughy man with a spiderweb of veins crocheted across his doorknob of a nose, was slumped forward in his pew and listing at a precarious angle, threatening at any moment to spill into the aisle; and the minister kept stealing nervous glances toward the front door, as if he expected it to combust at any moment. I readily assented to Shelly's demands.

Following the wedding, the party gathered in the backyard of the house we rented on Mapleton Avenue. We set stereo speakers in second-floor windows and spread picnic tables with food and drink—chips and dip, mini tacos, sausages in barbecue sauce, a beer keg, cheap wine, and cherry Kool-Aid laced with grain alcohol. The afternoon was warm, and people soon began dispensing with the trappings of formality. Ties hung from tree limbs, high heels lay scattered across the lawn, jackets had been strewn over chairs—the yard looked as though someone's luggage had exploded.

I met Billy by the beer keg.

"You're a lucky son of a bitch," he said, slapping me on the back and sloshing beer from his cup.

"Thanks, I know."

"I'm a lucky son of a bitch too," he said.

"How so?"

"Almost fried my ass in the field this morning. Left just before it caught fire."

I waved a fly from my shirtsleeve and tried to sound nonchalant. "You were up there?"

A sly grin creased Billy's face. "Yeah. Me and, what's her name, Shelly's cousin, took a little hike before the ceremony."

"Billy, she's fifteen. You came on to a high-school sophomore?"

"There's something about young girls," he said. "I don't know. They have sexual electricity. It makes my hair stand on end." His left leg began twitching. "They don't know what to do with it, where to take it. I'm like a guide."

"That's statutory rape," I lectured. "Were you smoking dope?"

"Just a taste, to smooth things out, you know?" His eyes were minnows darting through a shallow pool.

"Jesus, Billy, you almost burned down the forest."

"No, man, I'm sure it wasn't me." Billy's face contracted into a mass of horizontal creases, a study in concentration, as if he were straining to pull some memory from long, long ago, from a time when half the Earth still smoldered under molten lava. "It was probably a lightning strike or something," he said thoughtfully.

I looked up into an afternoon sky the color of a

robin's egg, shook my head, and walked toward Shelly, who was standing by the punch bowl. As I approached her, I noticed the circle of privacy people afforded her. She always attracted a group, but invariably they stood a step removed, as though they did not feel worthy to crowd too closely around her. They set her apart. Shelly had an allure defined not by her beauty, which she possessed in unfair abundance, nor by her charm, which she employed to her advantage seemingly without motive, but rather by an air of danger about her, a gorgeous recklessness that attracted people the way daredevils are attracted to free climbing or skydiving.

"What do women see in that guy?" I asked Shelly, jerking my head toward Billy.

She studied him for a moment. "He serves a purpose, and he's harmless. Think of him as a fence post with a penis. A handsome, dumb stick that doesn't require any attention at all except when you want to rub up against it, scratch a certain itch. Besides, he's your friend, remember?"

I would never have described Billy as a friend. He was the younger brother of a high-school classmate who had followed us to Boulder a few years after we all left for college. He took a class or two at school, never came close to passing, and hovered around the edges of life—waiting tables, selling a little marijuana, dropping by now and again to live for a week or two on the living-room couch.

He was just one of an assortment of human flotsam who seemed to drift through all college towns in those days.

The house on Mapleton Avenue collected the odd and the dispossessed. I always felt infused with a curious excitement while living there, like a kid visiting a carnival on the outskirts of town where men with bad teeth and tattooed forearms ran crooked games and where lumpy, tired-eyed women danced naked on a bare stage in a smoke-filled tent.

The house itself was a sprawling Victorian with high ceilings and wide, oak-framed vestibules. During the months leading up to our wedding, as well as for several months following it, Shelly and I shared a room that once must have been a reception parlor. It was large and breezy, with dormers, a fireplace, and wallpaper patterned with pale blue fleur-de-lis.

One bedroom upstairs was rented by Windship Universe, a bald waitress and sometimes street performer with a tranquil smile, a vacant gaze focused on some far horizon, and a predisposition to nudity. She was a sweet girl with an irritating outlook on life. To her, every event, from pedestrian to earth shattering, reflected the beautiful expression of cosmic will. Flat tire? Lost cat? Genocide in sub-Saharan Africa? Celestial karma, all. An exasperating, simplistic world view, but one I was more than willing to accommodate when, for example, she stood peeling carrots at the sink naked from pate to toe, naked and completely hairless—her head, eyebrows, armpits, pubes, legs all cleanly shaved. The absence of hair accentuated her nudity. An erotic nimbus glowed from her magnificent body. Carrots never tasted so good. Never before, never since.

Jeffrey Pugh, a meat eater and the ultimate primeval survivalist, sporadically occupied a second small room upstairs. He slept out back under a cottonwood most nights but came in during cold and snow; he likened it to early man seeking out the shelter of caves. He spent days on end wandering trails outside Boulder, and on occasion he would descend from the hills late in the evening with a yearling doe draped over his shoulders like a stole, its head rolling slowly in time to Jeffrey's loping gait, its tongue lolling from its dead mouth. He would hang it from his tree, skin it, gut it, slice a small piece of its liver and eat it raw, all the while chanting some nonsensical prayer to the gods of deer, thanking them for their sacrifice and promising to remember them to his children—as if any woman would willingly bear Jeffrey's offspring, ever. His breath reeked of dead flesh, he almost never bathed, and living creatures could often be seen making nests in the wild tangles of his hair. But his rent was paid regularly from a bank in Grand Junction, so we endured him and his money.

Two chemistry students whose names I do not remember but whom I referred to as "the twins" rented the basement. They were unremarkable except for their skittish manner, the faint sulfurous odor that sometimes wafted up from their room late at night, and their uncanny punctuality in emerging from their burrow whenever they sensed Windship roaming the upper regions free from the restraints of clothing.

How I ever became embroiled in such a strange mix confused me at times.

▶ ▶ ▶

During the summer following my first year of law school, I interned at a firm that performed occasional pro bono work in landlord disputes. Windship and Shelly had filed a complaint against the owner of the apartment they rented above the pottery studio where Shelly worked on east Pearl Street. It seemed he spent an inordinate amount of time tinkering around his property, often arriving unannounced and letting himself in with his master key. The plumbing constantly needed rooting, the bathtub caulking, the woodwork touching up.

On my initial visit to fact find for the firm, it became clear that Windship desperately wanted out of the lease. Apart from the irritation of having the landlord constantly underfoot, she had recently become involved with a Chinese exchange student who was schooled in feng shui and had convinced her that the apartment design was entirely incompatible with her aura.

"Window opens to the north," she told me when I arrived to fact find for the firm. "Entrance on the east," she added, pointing to the door and nodding affirmatively, as if that settled everything.

I explained to her as patiently as I could that bad feng shui vibes were not, to my knowledge, valid grounds for breaking a lease. I explained that a landlord had the right to regularly inspect his property and to perform required maintenance. Unable to ignore the fact that Windship was wearing nothing but a flimsy bathing suit cover-up under which no bathing suit resided, I also suggested that his visits would likely tail off if she remained fully clothed whenever he was present.

I was about to leave when Shelly walked through the front door and promptly rekindled my interest in pursuing their case. She was returning from climbing in Boulder Canyon. White chalk marks streaked her black tights and coated her hands. Her face bore rust-colored smudges from the rocks. Her hair, pulled into a tight ponytail, accented the sweep of her neck, the fullness of her lips. When I shook her hand, I noticed bloody knuckles and had to fight the almost uncontrollable urge to bring them to my mouth.

"Do what you can, won't you?" she asked. "We may not have much of a complaint, but we really are tired of this place. Too cramped. Need more space."

I promised I would do what I could.

Like the landlord, I found every excuse imaginable to visit Shelly. I filled a notebook with depositions. I inspected the owner's handiwork. I questioned tenants of other properties he owned, establishing that he rarely responded to their requests for maintenance. In short, I negotiated a release from their contract. When Shelly asked if I was interested in sharing a house she had located on the west side of town, I leapt at the opportunity to remain near her.

Our other housemates had also been of Shelly's choosing. Windship just naturally migrated with us. The twins had watched Windship perform "Howl" while standing in the fountain of the University of Colorado student center and had followed her home like stray puppies. Shelly thought they were cute and allowed them to stay. Jeffrey was a yin-yang decision: Shelly wanted a balance to Windship's otherworldliness and the twins' dazed scientific detachment. Jeffrey, oldest of our group and of unknown origin, grounded us in the tactile dirt-under-the-fingernails here and now. And Billy, the sometimes-present Billy, symbolized for us the ghost of past regrets and of future dread, a child-man who embodied at once a playful irresponsibility we secretly envied and the psychic seeds of failure we knew he would bring to germination as an adult. He was destined to remain suspended in that netherworld between youth and maturity, ill adjusted to either age, and we could all see it. He had a sad, hound-dog slope to his eyes that elicited sexual compliance from girls and uneasy commiseration among men.

As taken as I was with Shelly, I saw much less of her than I wished during those first halting days of courtship. She was forever off on one excursion or another: rock climbing in Eldorado Canyon, kayaking the white water of the Cache La Poudre, hiking the remote wilderness of Flattop Mountain. But when she was not away, Shelly allowed me to pursue her, and to this day I do not have the foggiest notion why. We were opposites: me a skinny, plain-featured, nonathletic pragmatist with my future laid out before me; she a beautiful, finely sculpted physical specimen without a plan in life other than to test its limits. I loathed the chaos of spontaneity; she thrived on it. I feared physical danger of any sort; she passionately sought it. Whenever I scolded her for her recklessness, for shooting rapids without wearing a life vest, for solo climbing without a rope, she would fix me with a genuinely puzzled expression.

"What fun would that be? To bob like a cork in the river? To tie myself to a rock? I might as well stay home and read a book."

She kept me off balance and uncomfortable, and for some reason I relished the disequilibrium. Just twenty-four, I had already planned out my life as straight and unswerving as the interstate bisecting the plains of eastern Colorado. I knew I would graduate law school in the top one-third of my class, work for a few years at the Boulder firm where I interned, develop a specialization in real estate, and spin off on my own once I had built a stable and reliable clientele. But Shelly was an unknown in my life's equation. She made me feel alive with expectation and anticipation. Other romances had always involved girls who wore coordinated outfits and who possessed cautious, balanced temperaments. Lovemaking had been satisfying but not impassioned, discourse interesting but not engrossing, companionship comfortable but not intimate. With Shelly, the world exploded anew each day, and I was intoxicated just being around her, living her exploits vicariously through her recounting. I spent weeks feeling as though I had just disembarked from a playground merry-go-round—disoriented, dizzy, and exhilarated.

When I proposed to her, she hesitated before answering, and she seemed to stiffen almost imperceptibly. Then her expression softened and her eyes teased mine. "Sure," she said, "that will be a trip to remember."

It really made no difference one way or the other to her whether or not we married. It was my idea. I believed the ceremony would seal our relationship. I felt certain Shelly had let me get as close to her as any man ever had, yet I sensed a gap remaining between us, a small span I could not bridge, a kind of Zeno's paradox between souls. I found the concept of two people symbolically joining as one enormously appealing.

▸ ▸ ▸

Following our marriage, life in the rambling old house took on a routine of sorts. I became somewhat inured to what was, looking back on it later from the objective distance of almost three decades, the rather bizarre everyday life swirling about me: dead game hanging from trees; naked men and women, Windship's friends, wandering the halls; Billy escorting one willing coed after another into unoccupied bedrooms for quick trysts. I could never shake the feeling of alienation from this group, however, like I was a stagehand in the midst of a Fellini dress rehearsal, and I soon became disenchanted with our living arrangements. I had graduated from law school and was cramming for the bar while holding down a clerkship at the firm in town. The house provided little privacy for serious study, and the parlor off the main hallway fell far short of my idea of a proper newlyweds' cottage.

I also grew weary of our roommates. The chemistry twins irritated the hell out of me when they loitered around the living room a bit too long watching Shelly practicing her yoga in a sleeveless tee and tights. She was oblivious to them, but I considered her contortions to be for my eyes alone. Jeffrey's bloodletting rituals increasingly concerned me. What I once considered an earthy individualism, I now judged psychopathic. Perhaps worst of all, Windship was gaining weight. I feared she might be pregnant, and I had no desire to witness her unblemished form distort and stretch before my eyes into the image of some naked fertility totem.

When I approached Shelly about moving, she was indifferent. I feared she might miss her friends, but she agreed without apparent regrets. That was the thing about Shelly: she exerted a gravitational pull; people were attracted to her. But although the planets require the sun to maintain their orbit, to keep from spinning crazily into space, the sun does not need the planets. Shelly was a friend to all but truly close to no one. As often as people sought her companionship, I never observed her seeking it from another. Therefore, when I suggested giving up the house, she simply asked, "When?"

That autumn, we moved to a small cabin in the hills above Boulder, up Sunshine Canyon, off a dirt road where dogs roamed freely and where the crop of choice in most backyard gardens was hemp. For a while, life was quiet in the hills, and serene. I often walked the meadow behind our cabin early in the morning, in the dim light before the sun rose above the low crest of the foothills to the east. Dry grass crunched under my boots from heavy frost, and my breath escaped in visible wisps as the meadow rose toward the dark line of aspen to the north. Many days, I followed a game trail to a rock outcropping and sat looking out over the Boulder valley, pale yellow in the early sun.

Our serenity was short lived. Shelly grew restless. Slow, meditative hikes were not a balm for her soul, but rather an irritant. She required action, movement. Time spent in idle contemplation was time away from living. She began staying overnight on her outings to the rivers and the canyons that offered greater challenges than the tame slopes surrounding our small valley. She always returned invigorated and lustful. Following an excursion, our lovemaking was always wild—an extension of her latest adventure, I sometimes felt. She would busy herself around the cabin for a few days following a trip but would soon be off again.

"I thought you would like it up here," I complained to her one evening. "I thought you loved the country."

"You don't know me," she answered without a hint of reproach.

"Tell me, then. Tell me who you are."

"I climb. I raft. I run. I ski. I love you. That's all there is about me."

"That doesn't help me understand."

"That's not my problem," she said, and walked out into the night.

By early spring, the old roommates started showing up. While sitting at the small table by the woodstove sipping coffee one morning, I saw Jeffrey stalking through the meadow. In the distance, he appeared even more threadbare than before, and he had grown a beard that extended halfway down his chest in scraggly tendrils. Shortly thereafter, small offerings to Shelly began showing up on the chopping block by the woodpile—a field-dressed rabbit or fox squirrel, a wreath of pinecones.

Windship, who turned out not to be pregnant but merely growing fat, would stay over for days at a time visiting with Shelly but having little to do with me. They would share intimate conversations long into the night curled up beneath the comforter on our bed while I slept fitfully on the couch in the front room.

One day in late March, Billy came by on the pretense of sharing some new strain of Southeast Asian hashish. He knew I had eased off the stuff since beginning to work for the law firm and knew also that Shelly rarely smoked anything at all. But he brought it by nonetheless and seemed disappointed when we refused to indulge with him. He ended up on a sleeping bag by the hearth for an extended stay. I began to worry in earnest when he hung his clothes in our small closet and arranged his pipes and rolling papers on the mantel.

When I confronted Shelly with my irritation and, yes, jealousy, she reacted with a calm detachment that infuriated me.

"I didn't ask these people over. But they should be welcome."

"I want you for myself. Is that so selfish?"

"Yes."

During the second week in April, a snowstorm moved in quietly during the night. I awoke on the couch just after dawn, sensing the storm rather than hearing it. Walking to the window, I watched thick flakes blanket the new grass in the meadow. Our fire had died during the night and Billy had neglected to stock the tinderbox as he said he would, so I put on a jacket, grabbed the ax by the kitchen door, went out into the cold morning, and walked to the woodpile. There on the chopping block was a small bouquet of early spring flowers: delicate yellow crocuses and small bunches of grape hyacinth. I suddenly felt the blood rush to my head. I whirled around with the ax raised to my shoulder, expecting to find Jeffrey crouching behind me, ready to lunge. No one was there, but I noticed trampled snow, and I followed a set of footprints around the cabin. They had paused at each window before circling back to our bedroom, where Shelly and Windship slept. I tried following the tracks into the woods, but the falling snow soon obscured them.

I returned to the cabin and, with some difficulty, lit a sputtering fire with the sodden wood. Turning my back to the hearth, I noticed Billy's empty sleeping bag. In the bedroom, I found Shelly, Windship, and Billy huddled together with the comforter pulled close around their chins.

Shelly smiled up at me. "Isn't the snow wonderful? Come. Get warm. Get out of those wet clothes. There's room here with us."

I walked back outside and up the meadow. Looking at the cabin from the edge of the woods through a fog of falling snow, I could see smoke rising in thick plumes from the stone chimney, billowing up from the cabin, as if it were engulfed in flames.

In the end, I was the one to move from the cabin into town. I wanted from Shelly what she could not give to me: a realignment of our solar system. I yearned to be the sun, to determine the orbit of her life, to define the limits of her arc through space. But, of course, the thought of a limiting influence was as foreign to Shelly as the thought of herself existing as mere matter apart from movement, apart from action. She needed always to feel the life force drumming within her, the wind ripping her from the comfortable perch, the wax on her wings beginning to melt. I loved the energy of her existence, but my inner core demanded I attempt to harness it, to direct its flow.

I remembered Shelly once cajoling me into gliding with her. She knew how to pilot a glider—was not certified, of course, but had flown dozens of times. An old friend at the airstrip towed us up from his bucking Piper and released us high above the plains just east of Boulder. Shelly flew in a few tight circles, getting accustomed to the controls, then pointed the glider west and searched out the thermals along the foothills. The rock outcroppings, like red fingers, stretched out for us as we swept past on rivers of warm air, our wing tips almost brushing the slopes, the shadow of our glider racing across treetops and meadows. I was dumb with fright, but Shelly was animated. Her eyes shone as if she were with fever. When shifting air currents jostled the glider, I reached forward in panic and grabbed her by the shoulders. Her skin was hot to the touch. This was Shelly; this was her sustenance.

▶ ▶ ▶

I saw little of the old crowd after Shelly and I separated. When the time came to open my law office, I moved to Denver and lost track of them. Boulder had grown more and more foreign to me over the years. A pedestrian walk sprang up along Pearl Street, and the pottery studio where Shelly used to work became a trendy fern bar. A communications consultant bought our old Victorian house on Mapleton Avenue and renovated it into a nouveau-West mansion. As with many university towns with their constant turnover of students, Boulder remained forever young while I aged. I retained little enthusiasm for a city that made me feel old at thirty.

The roommates and I were never close to begin with, and, in all objectivity, I had given them no reason to be. I had been possessive of Shelly from the start, aggressively challenging any rival for her attention. A constant undercurrent of cutthroat competition colored my relationship with the others.

Occasionally, however, I did hear of them. From a friend of a friend, I learned that Jeffrey spent time in the Veterans Administration hospital at Fort Logan and later took a job sorting mail in Broomfield. For months, I fully expected to see him featured on the local news. … "We interrupt regular programming to bring you this fast-breaking story. A hostage situation has developed at the Broomfield post office. An unidentified male worker … "

When insomnia used to banish me to the family room in the basement where I could putter about without disturbing my wife and sons, sometimes I would flip through the television channels and catch Windship on one of the local cable networks interviewing the latest guru du jour and hawking her series of self-realization videos (*Climb-*

ing That Stairway to Heaven, $19.95 each or the full five-tape set for $89.50; *The Zen of Sexual Self-Gratification*, $22.50 including the fully illustrated how-to guide). She had changed her name to Satayan, had grown a full head of blond hair, and was still beautiful in an Earth Mother sort of way.

And what of Billy? Billy finally outgrew his attraction to schoolgirls. He fell completely under Shelly's spell and followed her around for years, like a personal valet. I do not know if they ever developed a physical relationship, but he faithfully tagged along wherever Shelly's whim directed her: trekking in Nepal, backpacking in Central America, surfing in Australia. I usually received postcards or pictures from him, but his last correspondence was a short letter from Cape Hatteras, North Carolina, that included a newspaper clipping concerning Shelly.

"Of all places," the letter started, "all she wanted was to see a hurricane up close. She has been in places a hundred times more dangerous than here. I don't get it."

The newspaper article contained the facts of Shelly's death, the simply enumerated details of time and place.

She had been found naked, washed up on the beach. An elderly couple out collecting shells in the aftermath of the hurricane had stumbled upon her body partially covered with sand and festooned with seaweed and devil's purses. Because she was without suspicious marks or injuries, and because the autopsy determined the cause of death as drowning, the reporter speculated that the wild surf had ripped off her bathing suit and deposited her on the beach with the detritus of the storm.

"She may have been wading in the surf and been bowled over by a wave," one local official was quoted as saying. "Tourists forget the undertow," he continued. "They are knee deep in the water one second and gone the next. Don't mean to be doing nothing dangerous, just get caught unawares."

I knew better; Shelly had known exactly what she was doing. I closed my eyes and clutched the news clip to my chest and I saw it all: Shelly was standing on a sand dune late at night watching the broad expanse of moonlight dance over the black sea, the white foam of the surf breaking in the distance sparkling like champagne foam. The air was moist and humid, the hurricane still a hundred miles southeast, the raging surf the only evidence that a storm was imminent. A pair of dolphins arched in the flat surface of the trough between the break line and the beach, the smooth leather of their skin glistening. And suddenly she needed to be enfolded in the warm saline currents, ached to feel the life of the sea ebbing and flowing around her, within her, craved the equilibrium between her own life fluids and those of the liquid world spread before her. So she stripped off her clothes and danced into the ocean, glided through the calm waters to the breaking surf, and somehow struggled through the roiling crests until she found herself in the cold swells seaward of the outer sandbar floating over deep water while the subtle tug of the Gulf Stream seduced her out farther and farther until she realized where she was and she looked back toward shore where the cottage lights along the coast looked like a thin yellow thread against black velvet and she rolled over on her back and treaded water and laughed up at the gibbous moon hanging low in the sky like a lopsided plate and at the stars dropping into the ocean so close on the horizon she actually reached out for one and she realized she was close to home now and she said, "This will be a trip to remember," and she was swallowed by the rising storm.

My initial reaction to Shelly's death was not of mourning but of relief. I no longer loved her, had not even thought of her often in recent years. I knew from the time I left her that she would have been too much trouble to put up with, that she would have been one heartache after another, mystery after mystery. She would never have allowed me a normal life. But I did still admire the memory of her beauty and her spirit. Her death ensured that that image would remain frozen in time, unthreatened by the conspiracies of age that rob vitality and appearance. I recalled someone once saying that by age fifty we all finally have the face we deserve, and I was relieved that Shelly had died before her past caught up with her. But then I thought, *You son of a bitch*, and I suddenly found myself weeping, weeping in part for Shelly, and perhaps a little for Jeffrey and Windship and Billy, but mostly for myself.

Windship Universe
Floats to Earth

When the lady elbowed ahead of her in the checkout line, Satayan's first impulse was to put the small discourtesy into cosmic perspective, an almost imperceptible annoyance, the brush of a jellyfish against the broad back of God. Let it pass.

The lady turned to Satayan in a fluster. "I just have a few things; I'm sure you don't mind. Such a rush. Company."

Roughly the same age as Satayan, around fifty, she wore an elegant black dress that showed to advantage her medically reconfigured body: breasts that defied gravity, stomach without fold or paunch, skin stretched so tightly across her forehead, it appeared as if she might split to the touch, like an overripe tomato. Her cart was stuffed to overflowing: two trays of frozen hors d'oeuvres, a dozen eggs, a pint of heavy cream, a bottle of multivitamins plus

▶

iron plus calcium plus selenium, a loaf of Jewish rye, a large bag of coffee beans, assorted wedges of imported cheese, and a scented bathroom deodorizer, Summer Breeze. Satayan's own basket contained a liter of spring water and half a cantaloupe, soft almost to the point of spoilage, marked half price.

"Go ahead," Satayan answered. "I can see you are conflicted. Your lower chakras are definitely dominating."

"My what?"

"Your astral tube is blocked in your lower planes. From the looks of you, I'd say between your swadhisthana and manipura chakras."

Although the woman's negativity had severely weakened her energy field, Satayan's experienced eye detected a faint aura, thin as an eggshell, outlining her head. The aura was murky and dark, like burnt curry, sure indications of a quarrelsome, ill-tempered disposition.

"Where? What? Are you speaking English?"

"Your spiritual energy is centered between your navel and your genitalia."

The woman winced as though she had been pinched in just such a location. "Listen, just forget I asked, okay?" She turned her back and began unloading her groceries onto the conveyor belt.

Satayan attempted to ignore this latest rudeness. She took a deep, cleansing breath and turned her mind inward to the image of a vast meadow bursting with daffodils, one lone blossom, this harried and unthinking shopper, wilting and brown among the millions of flowers. She drew into her consciousness the expanse of color, the bright yellow sea set against a faultless sky as wide as the universe, the blue and yellow that filled her vision only two small flecks in the eye of the Divine One. But slowly, persistently, her focus narrowed back to that single withered bloom, that one mar on perfection's landscape. She could not shrug off the bite of anger growing within her. *It is not the way of the enlightened to harbor ill will toward anyone or anything*, she lectured herself. *A nonjudgmental mind is open to serenity.* Her outward countenance remained placid, an enigmatic half smile adorning a face uncreased by concern. But her mind buzzed.

Bad karma? she wondered. She realized that the fans who recognized her, either from her infomercials or from the old days when she knew herself as Windship Universe and interpreted astrological charts on a cable show, thought she had it made. They often wrote to her of their problems, of relationships gone sour, of jobs without promise. They envied how together she appeared, calm and controlled. They had no idea how difficult it was to keep the focus on the horizon, to ignore the little annoyances that every day threatened to distract her. Like this artificial, offensive woman in line.

The checkout girl, thin as a celery stalk and wearing an expression similar to that of the cod displayed on ice in the seafood section, studied the items the lady in the black evening dress had placed on the counter. "Express line. Six-item limit."

The woman set her feet as if she were bracing against a gale, planted her jewel-bedecked fist on her hip, and fixed the cashier with a stare that could melt wax. "You do not want to start with me, I assure you. Just ring up the groceries."

The girl peered back, slack jawed. "Sorry. Can't. Not without my supervisor's okay."

"Then you had better call him, because I'm not moving."

Another shopper lined up behind Satayan and gave her the sideways glance of recognition. She was a large woman and wore a mismatched sweat suit. Hair curlers poked indiscreetly from under a scarf depicting Guantanamo Bay in lime green and orange. "I have one of your yoga tapes," she said softly to Satayan. "It's helped me so much. After the surgery and all."

Satayan gave her a pat on the forearm and a sincere smile. "I'm so pleased to hear that. Thank you."

She was accustomed to strangers approaching her with unsolicited testimonials. Those who watched her shows or attended her workshops instinctively liked her, trusted her, now even more than earlier in her career. When she was young, the fan letters came mostly from men and were solicitous and propositional. She had been beautiful, lithe, and sensual, with the long, limber body of a dancer. But the yeast of age had softened her features and filled in the high cheekbones, had rounded the sharp curves so that now she appeared more comforting than alluring, more dependable than tempting. One current admirer, a middle-aged woman like herself, wrote that Satayan possessed a face like freshly baked bread—warm and nourishing. So now they trusted her advice and trusted her authenticity. She was caring yet aloof to worldly distractions, the irritations that rippled the still waters of the soul. And Satayan genuinely did care for the well-being of her devotees. But they had no clue about her.

The woman in curlers noticed the two in standoff ahead of them in line. "Honey, the sign does say Six-Item Limit. Why not just hop over to the next line? No one's there."

"Why don't you just hop back to the farm, you cow," answered the lady in the black dress.

The checkout girl hit the call button for her supervisor.

And just how did Satayan react to this small conflict rapidly escalating before her eyes? Well, she began to flex the finely honed muscles of disassociation she had trained so diligently to develop. Satayan, formerly Windship Universe, formerly Ellen Fortunato of San Diego, California, gazed off into the distance and attempted to calm her mind from growing ever more agitated. ...

She remembered back to the day she had become one with the universe. She was sixteen, studying in the recreation room of the hacienda-style stucco in the foothills above Lemon Grove that her mother had purchased with partial proceeds from the divorce settlement. Her biology book lay open on her lap to a transparency of protozoan soup, minute organisms swimming in a drop of pond water. Ellen's left hand held a pencil, which she absently drummed against her thigh. With her right index finger, she wrapped loose strands of blond hair into tight curls. Her eyes wandered from the page. She noticed that the rubber plant in the large pottery container beside her beanbag chair was sprouting new growth. Five shiny leaves spread like an open palm from a long, thin stem. It resembled an arm raised in greeting, hand waving, fingers spread wide. Ellen raised her own hand in response, spread her own fingers, and gently caressed the leaves arching toward her. Suddenly, it occurred to her that the rubber plant and she were growing by exactly the same process: both just a mass of cells dividing and dividing and dividing again. She and the plant and the fly that buzzed around her bottle of Coke, all the same. ...

So long ago, Satayan thought, standing in the grocery

line. *A different lifetime, another world.*

"What seems to be the problem here?" asked a man who, according to his How May I Serve You Today button, was named Bob R.

"Over limit," explained the countergirl.

The lady in the evening dress relaxed her posture and directed a come-hither-if-only-you-were-not-on-duty smile at the supervisor. Her freshly capped teeth sparkled like pearls. "There seems to have been the most minor of misunderstandings," she explained. "I'm in such a rush." False eyelashes fluttered.

Bob R. turned to the checkout girl. "I think we can make an exception this once, don't you, Juanita?"

"Whatever."

Bob R. retreated into a glass-walled office as Juanita scanned the grocery items. The lady in black retrieved a discount coupon from her sequined bag and handed it to the clerk. Twenty percent off the air freshener—forty-eight cents.

"Expired," Junaita said.

"Call back your supervisor, you moron," spat the lady.

"That is unkind," said the woman in curlers. "You should take a lesson from her," she said, and nodded toward Satayan.

"Who?" questioned the lady in black. "This Earth

Mother reject from the sixties?"

Satayan's pensive smile tightened ever so slightly; the muscles of her jaw twitched almost imperceptibly. *It's true,* she thought. *Left this world on a warm autumn day in 1965 and began the ascent to a higher plane. Being in this world by abandoning it. Addition by subtraction. Did it work any longer?* Satayan wondered. She seemed so alienated from turn-of-the-millennium sensibilities, the second-nature rudeness one person showed another, the complete absence of grace. *Was there still a place for her? If not, so? Any worse stuck three decades back than to have evolved with the times into this egocentric, vitriolic monument to self-absorption standing before her?*

Satayan rarely harbored ill thoughts about anyone— her psychic powers were sufficiently advanced that she feared the mere wish of bad fortune might make it so. Her normal reaction to hostility was aikido-like, to move with the flow, to use the inertia of attack to guide it away from her. Passive resistance or, more commonly, passive retreat. Years ago, when her mother had confronted her about her eccentric behavior ("I will not have you embarrass me in front of the entire town"), Satayan had retired to her room to meditate for three days. When schoolmates mocked her, she had found escape in a mystical world they could not inhabit—the *I Ching*, the *Book of the Dead*, the Celtic penitentials, any alternative universe where normal was turned on its head and fleeting dreams were as firm as stone. But in the case of this woman, Satayan's instinct turned to aggression. Still, she felt more comfortable in retreat.

Satayan had endured insults all her life, suffered the taunting comments, the derisive stares, the disenfranchisement of family, all with benign resignation. Why did this particular person agitate her so? Perhaps it was not this one woman, but rather the cumulative weight of all past rejections she now felt, the yoke of negativity finally buckling her knees. She felt heavy, cumbersome, and defeated. And something more welled within her—anger. How dare this woman and others of her cloth impose their collective burden on her?

"What is it this time, Juanita?" Bob R. asked, his voice betraying annoyance. Juanita silently handed him the expired coupon.

The lady in line smiled demurely. "Your checkout girl is being very difficult. Perhaps she doesn't understand her responsibilities. Has she been in this country for long?"

Juanita glared at the woman in black. "Listen, *puta*, I'll—"

"Juanita, just ring up the discount, will you, and get the line moving."

Bob R. turned to the woman, said, "Sorry," whirled around, and once again went back to his office.

Juanita bagged the groceries.

The lady in black dug through her purse and held out her credit card.

Juanita stared dumbly at it. She glanced briefly at Bob R.'s door, then at Satayan, then back to the woman. "No credit cards. Cash or check only."

"That does it, you idiot!" The lady screamed. "Bob! Bob!"

Bob R. charged from the office.

"Bob, I want this wetback out of my sight. Get her back across the border where she belongs, and get my bags into the car this instant."

The woman in curlers said, "You should apologize right now" and took a step toward the lady in black, crowding Satayan, so that the three stood in a tight ball between the counter and the guide rail.

Satayan touched the woman gently on her elbow. "You do seem to have issues."

"Issues?" The lady jerked her arm from Satayan and wheeled to face her. "My only issues are an incompetent clerk, a fat slob trying to tell me what to do, and a spaced-out hippie." The lady looked aggressively at Satayan, but after a moment, the pinched anger of her mouth relaxed into a sneer. "I recognize you now. My ex-husband used to watch you on channel thirty-one. A yoga show. He had great fun with you, howling at the screen while you twisted and flopped about in that leotard. He kept expecting you to spill out of it."

Satayan reddened and focused on the floor. *Concentrate on the tile,* she told herself.

"Tell me," the woman in black continued, "didn't you realize why people watched? Weren't you embarrassed? Wasn't your family humiliated?"

Focus on the detail, Satayan told herself. *Clear your thoughts.* Her mind reeled, ticking through techniques: breath control, silent chanting, visualization, projection, channeling. She concentrated with all her effort on the tile, a brown triangle, its yellow-wax finish specked with gold. *Center on the tile.* But her eyes wandered. *On the red of the shopping basket, concentrate. Meditate on the cantaloupe. Focus on the cantaloupe half, its soul split open like a wound. Breathe. Center. The cantaloupe. The cratered moonscape of its rind. The vacant, mournful hollow where seeds once nested. The overripe orange flesh, soft, beckoning, seductive.*

Satayan reached into her cart and slowly removed the cellophane wrapping from the fruit. She lifted it to her nose. The pungent sweetness of it assaulted her senses like an old memory. She turned it in her hand, feeling its heft, appreciating its symmetry. Then, ever so slowly, with deliberation and conviction, she crowned the woman in the black evening gown. Satayan screwed the cantaloupe onto the lady's skull as if she were juicing a lemon. Orange pulp ribboned the woman's hair and decorated the lovely formfitting dress. Sticky dribbles etched shallow furrows through thick makeup.

"Oh, my," said the woman in the sweat suit.

"Yes!" said Juanita.

The woman in black opened her mouth, but her words stuck in her throat. She emitted only a croaking sound, a hoarse, guttural exhale. She took a half step backward and opened her eyes wide in disbelief. Then she turned and, cantaloupe still perched atop her head, stumbled toward the exit.

Bob R. refused to see anything going on around him. He called to the woman, "Have a nice day!" and walked to his office wearing the vacant smile of a simpleton.

And Satayan—what of Satayan? Following the coronation, she began to feel light-headed, or rather, more literally, her head began feeling lighter. She sensed her body losing mass, her limbs growing buoyant and unsubstantial, energy replacing matter, until, before long, she became weightless and slowly levitated from the floor. She floated. She drifted around the store, gliding through the aisles, over the frozen foods, over the canned vegetables. She watched the lady in black stagger from the grocery and smiled down at Juanita and the woman in sweats who stared up at her with mouths agape, hopping in place, as if they too were about to take flight. When Satayan alighted in the spot she had left only a few moments earlier, she felt a bit more solid than before, felt firmly grounded, as if gravity were hugging her more tightly to Earth's breast. But her spirit remained light and floating. Her spirit still soared.

Migration Patterns

Regaining Flight

When birds start raining from the sky, a vision flashes through Wes's mind of some biblical prophecy, a plague loosed upon the Earth. He thinks back to his Sunday-school days—there were frogs and gnats and locusts, but he remembers nothing about birds.

Driving along the frontage road, he watches a flock of Canada geese lurch unsteadily from the low clouds, bank clumsily, and hit the ground with a bounce. Some waddle around, wings flapping, as though still aloft; others appear stunned, hunkering down, heads bobbing on rubbery necks. Wrens spin to the earth in heaps of brown feathers, dotting the stubble field off to the west. A merganser nose-dives onto his hood. Bioterrorism? A natural thought, given the times, but he dismisses the idea quickly because it seems only birds are afflicted.

Because he grew up on a ranch in western Colorado, Wes is seldom surprised by nature's practical jokes. He has

▶

seen a haystack spontaneously burst into flame; a coyote mate with his best hunting dog; a pig eat its young; his grandfather, two days dead and laid out in the parlor for viewing, sit straight up in his coffin and belch before settling back into his final rest. So Wes is not shocked by what he sees unfolding before him, but he is curious. He had been headed to the Stop-N-Go for a six-pack, a bag of pretzels, and a rope or two of beef jerky, his usual Friday-evening fare during these lean and solitary days, but he slides his truck to a stop on the glazed street and turns back toward the clinic, where he had dropped off his black lab, Ishmael, earlier in the day for his latest round of chemotherapy.

Wes does not especially like the new veterinarian, Gretchen, the one who acquired the practice when her predecessor retired south to Tucson last year. She talks with that clipped northeastern accent that sounds reserved and foreign. And she is not his type. Easy enough on the eyes, sure, but on the tall side, almost as tall as he, with the sinewy, long muscles of a ranch hand. What he would call competent looking, capable of taking care of herself. And a bit too blunt for his taste, not afraid to call you on it when you begin shooting the breeze on topics you know nothing about, even if you are just trying to make conversation. But she is a vet, the logical person to look to for answers.

It is sleeting hard when Wes pulls into the lot of Gretchen's clinic and parks beneath the green neon sign advertising Holistic Pet Services—another reason he does not particularly care for her. She prescribes acupuncture for animals, deep-muscle massage for her "geriatric" patients, and other treatments Wes finds absolutely baffling: computer-microchip identification implants, laser surgery, something called ultrasonography diagnostics. She has little pamphlets in her waiting room with titles such as "Dental Hygiene for Your Best Friend" and "Stay Connected to Your Pet—Webcam 24 Hours a Day."

Where Wes comes from, a sick yard dog or barn cat is as likely to be taken on a one-way trip to the backcountry as to a vet. Although he would never consider putting down Ishmael, he does not understand people who brush their dog's teeth, or how someone as no-nonsense as Gretchen can buy into such ideas. Once, when he had attempted to call her on it, tease her a little, give her a friendly ribbing, she had cut him short by stuffing his pockets with several of the brochures. "Read first," she had lectured him, "before you criticize."

Wes leans his shoulder into the truck door to open it against a wind blowing hard from the north. *Straight down the chute*, he thinks, *nothing between the frozen tundra and Colorado except the flat shelves of eastern Montana and Wyoming*. He sees Gretchen kneeling in the wet grass of the large-animal corral behind the clinic and, pulling the wide brim of his hat down low against the storm, walks over to join her. Near the back of the parking lot, he loses all traction on the slick asphalt and skates the last ten feet, arms flapping like one of the downed geese. Gretchen is using a hand towel to massage what appears to be a meadowlark, gently stroking its feathers.

Approaching the crippled bird, Wes becomes cautious. "Should you be handling that thing without gloves?"

"Just grab another towel, find a bird, and start warming it."

Birds continue to fall: robins flutter down like badminton shuttlecocks, a clutch of magpies hop across the parking lot, a red-tailed hawk preens over by a gnarled cottonwood. Wes approaches the hawk but thinks better of it when he considers the angry beak and stilettolike talons. He ignores it in favor of a chickadee or some such seedeater, which he bundles in his towel, careful not to touch its feathers with his bare hands. He carries it at arms' length back to Gretchen.

"What the hell is going on with these things?"

"Ice."

"Ice? We're not talking a poison cloud here, an epidemic or something?"

Gretchen looks up at him dismissively. "Ice. Their wings ice up, like with airplanes, and they lose flight. The larger species should be fine; their body heat will warm them soon enough. The smaller ones need our help to thaw out."

Gretchen carries the meadowlark to the clinic while Wes follows with his own tiny package. Inside, she has positioned a large wire cage in the center of her waiting room with desk lamps at either end as warmers. The heat is turned up and has caused the front window to fog over.

"I'll be damned," Wes says, placing the chickadee into the cage along with a few dozen other birds that are already flitting about, testing their wings. The room is dim, except for the warming lamps, so the birds appear to be onstage, ready to perform. "You have a regular melting pot of the bird kingdom here."

Gretchen ignores him. "I've heard of this happening back East," she says, "but never this far west, and never this early in the year."

She pronounces *back* like *Bach*, and Wes finds himself irritated with her. "It's this screwed-up weather," he pronounces with the conviction of a native and with a tone that implicates Gretchen, implies somehow that she is responsible, that the low-pressure systems have stalked her migration from Boston, east to west, a reversal of the laws of nature. Like birds falling from the sky.

And, in fact, winter had come early that year to his part of the country. September brought a hard freeze that had blackened aspen leaves on the branch. Early snow in the high country had driven elk from the forests onto suburban golf courses searching for open grazing. Black bears had ransacked garbage bins in commuter neighborhoods dotting the foothills west of Denver. And now, by mid-October, a gray half-light usually reserved for February has settled in.

The sudden transition to winter had caught Wes off guard, left him on edge. His dog, Ishmael, had seemed unnerved as well. He took to whining—whining to be let out, whining almost immediately to be let back in. At night, he wandered the house, restless and jumpy, growling at the faintest disturbance—a train's whistle two miles distant, a fox rustling through the dry skeleton of the vegetable garden, a branch creaking against a gutter.

Only after Ishmael began limping badly and quit his feed altogether had Wes stopped blaming the weather for his dog's behavior and taken him to Gretchen's clinic. Two, three visits, tests, cancer. He did not understand all of the technical language she used to explain Ishmael's condition, only that he was in some danger and that aggressive treatment was called for. Because of the prognosis and the cost involved, she suggested euthanasia as one option. Wes settled instead on a regime of chemotherapy and acupuncture and both despised Gretchen for her cool clinical diagnosis and admired her for her tender handling of his dog once his decision had been made.

"Let's collect another batch," Gretchen says.

"Just ice, right? Nothing contagious?"

"Don't be absurd," she says, eyes flashing anger for an instant, and then relaxing. "Sorry. Don't mean to snap. I could really use some help."

They go out into the storm and return a half dozen times until the birds in the immediate vicinity of the clinic are accounted for. Wes is relieved to see that the hawk has regained flight and is now perched high in the cottonwood, looking down on them like a disapproving judge.

Back inside the clinic, they are both wet to the skin, and although Gretchen wears a hooded slicker, her hair is plastered to her head and neck. She peels off her jacket and begins drying her hair with one of the leftover towels. Wes appreciates the easy naturalness of her actions—without a hint of self-consciousness, head tilted to one side, hair the color of cinnamon taken into the fold of her towel. He locks onto a fleeting image of Gretchen emerging from her morning shower and repeating just such a routine.

Wes shakes the water from his hat as he shakes the image from his mind. "That about do it?" he asks.

"For here. Think I'll drive out to the lake and check on the migratory birds. Make sure they are not in danger."

"I hadn't planned on making a night of it with the fowl," Wes says.

"No one asked you to. I'll be fine. Let's take a peek at Ishmael before I head out. You may be able to take him home."

They walk to a small enclosure to the side of the main kennel where Ishmael rests on a padded mat, recovering from his latest treatment. When they enter, his tail slaps the mat and he lifts his head but does not rise.

"How's my boy?" Wes asks, kneeling and rubbing the lab's muzzle. "How's my fella?"

"A little tired," Gretchen answers for Ishmael. "A little worn out from the chemotherapy. But you'll pick up, won't you, boy?" She scratches behind his ear, then straightens and walks to the door.

"If it's okay, I'll hang around a while," Wes says.

"Sure," Gretchen says. "You can leave him here tonight or take him home, your call. Just be sure the door is locked when you're done. Someone got into my drug cabinet last month. And leave the lamps on beside the bird pen. I'll be back to release them after the worst of this is past."

She goes, and Wes sits and cradles Ishmael's head in his lap, stroking his flank, noting the milky flatness in the dog's eyes.

Wes bought Ishmael three years ago to help fill an empty house after he and Lynn Ann finally called it quits. She had moved back to the Western Slope, to a world of sagebrush and rodeos and uncomplicated men with predictable concerns: weather, livestock, land, trucks. She had accused Wes of losing his roots. And who was he to argue? First of his family to graduate college, a construction-management job in Denver that kept him at a desk as much as in the field, neckties hanging in his closet.

Still, their breakup had flattened him. Together since high school, they had fallen in love, then spent the next fifteen years gliding out of it, gliding on so gentle an angle of descent, they had hardly felt the impact with the ground. Lynn Ann had been first to register the jolt, and it saddened Wes that neither of them could gather the energy to attempt reviving what they once had.

The puppy provided a distraction from his hurt. Wes took Ishmael along when he visited construction jobs. While he reviewed time sheets and schedule margins, Ishmael chased prairie dogs that had managed to escape the earthmover's blade. They would drive for hours through the leathery Colorado countryside, Wes carrying on a one-sided conversation, Ishmael riding shotgun, lapping up every word.

As the months passed and Wes eventually began dating again, his dog proved a reliable judge of female compatibility. If Ishmael took to Wes's date, Wes got along with her as well. If Ishmael shied away, Wes invariably developed reservations of his own. Only twice had Wes ignored Ishmael's guidance: Pamela had been the first,

Gretchen the second.

Pamela had been Wes's attempt to right his world turned on its head. She was the polar opposite of his ex-wife, which made her irresistible to Wes, even though Ishmael would slink from the room whenever she entered. Born and raised in Los Angeles, she was stunning, hip, and savvy. Lynn Ann was dark complexioned, Pamela fair. Lynn Ann was serious and level headed, Pamela bubbly and mercurial. Pamela considered Denver to be a cow town beyond redemption and was there only to further her career as Sunny Lane, the television weather and traffic girl. Although she was attracted to Wesley (she always called him by his full given name), she refused to be seen riding in his truck. She banished his Stetson to the top shelf of the hall closet, and she dressed him upscale from the trendy shops, mainly in shades of charcoal and gray. And she had suggested more than once that he would do well to sell the five-acre horse property he and Lynn Ann had bought twenty miles south of Denver and move to a loft in the city. He could find a nice family to adopt Ishmael, a family with kids.

Wes had ended it quickly last summer when Pamela finally insisted he choose between her and his dog. A simple matter, really. She had left him with what for her must have been the ultimate insult: "I guess it's true, Wesley. You can never take the country out of the boy."

And who was he to argue? He loved his truck, his dog, his land, where he could rise early and watch the yellow-dusted finches dart among the branches of the apple trees as dawn spread across an eastern horizon uncluttered by city skylines.

Yes, Wes thinks as he gently eases away from a now-sleeping Ishmael, *I should have listened to him. Would have saved a lot of time and a little pain.*

Outside the clinic, night has fallen and snowflakes as large as pearl buttons begin to mix with the sleet, catching the light thrown from the street lamps and the headlights of passing cars. Wes gets into his truck and allows the engine to warm for a minute or two before beginning his drive home. Pulling gingerly from the parking lot onto the road, he notices ice accumulating on the power lines overhead, stalactitelike fangs hanging from cables that sway in the wind. He engages the four-wheel drive, but his truck still feels light on the street, the back end threatening to fishtail with every turn. He flips on the radio to catch the weather alerts and hears a report from the state wildlife department about the situation with the birds. As he drives backstreets through the neighborhoods toward his place, he notices people out in their yards, darkly bundled shapes moving ghostlike through the fog. They carry garden rakes to knock ice and snow from trees still weighted with leaves, and they haul around cardboard boxes to collect the grounded birds. Children run across the white lawns peering under shrubbery and into the shadows of the trees.

Wes suddenly aches to be a part of that scene—he and Ishmael and some woman whose face and form he cannot bring into focus, perhaps a kid or two, out in the snow, a warm fire waiting inside. But after Pamela, Wes had given up on long-term relationships, had pushed aside the thought of replacing Lynn Ann in his heart and in his bed. That is why he had resisted Ishmael's signal when the dog absolutely mooned over Gretchen during their first visit to the clinic. Then, during their second appointment, Wes quickly backed off when she declined his invitation to discuss Ishmael's case during dinner.

"I don't think so," Gretchen had said. "Getting involved with clients, not a good idea."

"Whoa, there. I wasn't proposing marriage, just a cheeseburger or something."

"No, thanks. I'm sure you understand."

"Sure, right. No big deal. It's just that my dog is a pretty good judge of character, so I thought, you know … "

"Coming from Ishmael, I take that as a compliment," she had said while rumpling the dog's ears in her hands.

But now, driving through the storm, Wes grieves that no one is waiting for him at home. He regrets his decision to let Ishmael rest overnight at the clinic, and he wishes to be among company. He turns into a small strip mall and stops at a local tavern, one of those places tucked into the suburbs that caters to a regular clientele dropping in after work for a drink or for a quick bite when they do not feel like cooking—upscale burgers, oven-fired personal pizzas. Two televisions frame the bar, stock-car racing on one, some kind of pro-wrestling smack down on the other. The hum of the top twenty drifts over the room like a cloud of tobacco smoke.

The place is crowded, even with the storm building outside. It is Friday evening, after all. He finds a stool at the end of the bar and nurses a beer and remembers back two weeks earlier when he had run into Gretchen at this very place. She had come in with two couples and taken a wraparound corner booth. One couple must have been an item. They sat shoulder to shoulder, and Wes noticed the man's hand resting high on the woman's thigh. The other pair seemed younger than the first and more tentative together, the girl jittery with her hands, the man glancing around the busy room as he talked to her. Gretchen appeared to be friends with both couples, perhaps the organizer of their little get-together. She was animated in conversation, laughing easily and often. Her hair was pulled up off of her neck, and she wore tight jeans and a knit top that showed to advantage her athletic build.

Later in the evening, feigning surprise, Wes had intercepted her as she returned from the bathroom. "So, animal docs do take off their lab coats every once in a while."

"Occasionally. I was wondering if you were ever going to come say hello or just stay hunched over your beer all evening."

Had Wes noticed something in her voice? A softening? An invitation? "I didn't want to disturb you, and I haven't been much for conversation lately, what with Ishmael's trouble."

"We're doing everything we can," Gretchen had tried to reassure him. "Keep positive. Keep thinking good thoughts."

Wes motioned to the table with the neck of his beer bottle. "It's none of my business, but no man in your life? Have you sworn off them?"

Gretchen followed his glance and did not answer for a moment, as if she were weighing the consequence of shooting straight or deflecting the question with impersonal generalizations. Gretchen basically was a straight shooter. "You're right, it's none of your business. But let me ask you something. Do you think a person in her right mind would pull up stakes and move halfway across the country for no reason other than a change of scenery?" She hesitated and looked at him for a moment, started to speak again, but held back, as if silently calculating the pros and cons of some decision, then added, "I'm not ready to complicate my life again."

She returned to her table, and Wes finished his beer and left the bar feeling more alone than ever.

He feels that same emptiness now, even though Gretchen is not in the pub, and he feels a growing irritation with her again, as if she were to blame for his loneliness. *No, she is out in weather she has no business in, tromping around an unfamiliar countryside, a countryside that charges a high price for ignorance when nature turns ugly. Well, that's her problem,* Wes thinks as he lays a five on the bar countertop and walks back outside.

The storm has thickened while Wes was in the pub, has taken on body and force. Back on the road, driving now takes all of Wes's concentration. The snow flashing in his headlights becomes almost hypnotically blinding. He listens to reports of the interstate being closed east to Limon because of ground blizzards. The state patrol asks that people stay home, travel only for emergencies.

The snow blows horizontally, coating the north side of trees, laying down a white sheet over the ice on the road. Wes notices a power cable down and the houses gone dark for a half-mile stretch to the west. He slows for the turnoff leading to his property but slides past. He begins to back up, thinks again of Gretchen ten miles east at the reservoir, curses under his breath, shifts into first gear, and drives east toward the lake.

The two-lane blacktop dips and curves through four miles of humpbacked prairie before leveling out to follow the fence posts and irrigation ditches that dissect the table-flat landscape east of the city. On open plains, the storm turns from liquid to solid. What had been a swirling mix of wind and sleet and snow comes together as a wall that limits Wes's vision to the few feet in front of him that his truck's headlights carve out of the whiteness. His grip tightens on the wheel and a knot as hard as a fist forms in his gut. Occasionally, another set of lights inches toward him and he slows almost to a halt, studying the vehicles headed back into town, hoping to see Gretchen. But she does not pass, and his worry accumulates with the snow.

A few miles farther along, he stops to help a compact car that has spun off the road, cut through a barbed-wire fence, and come to rest in a field. A tow truck idles beside the compact, and a large man wearing a yellow slicker and thick khaki overalls is hooking the winch cable from the truck to the automobile's front bumper.

"Got things under control?" Wes shouts to the trucker.

A man with a lightweight trench coat stands to the side of the road sucking on a cigar. "Yeah." The trucker hitches a thumb over his shoulder toward the man. "I'd make a pretty fair living if there was more like him around. Taking a little bit of tin out in this mess." The driver straightens with a grunt. "You might want to think about following me and the fool on in. Don't want to be caught if it turns for the worse."

"Thanks," Wes says, "but I'm out looking for my own fool." Wes climbs back into his truck and continues on.

It takes nearly an hour to crawl the ten miles to the lake. As he crosses the cattle guard marking the entrance to the state park surrounding the reservoir, Wes spots Gretchen's car nose down in a roadside drainage ditch. The car is empty. He scans the middle distances for any sign of her. Unless the elements are playing tricks on his senses, the storm appears to be lifting just a bit, the wind pushing it southeast toward the Okalahoma panhandle.

The snow lets up enough that Wes can make out a cloud of fog rising above the still-unfrozen lake, and he starts across the field. Tufts of coarse prairie grass poke through the snow that squeaks beneath his boots, and he has to watch his step to keep from stumbling on the uneven terrain. When he looks up to regain his bearings, the tree line at water's edge comes into view, a shadow against a lighter night sky, and, below that, the dark silhouette of a person moving among the trees.

By the time he reaches her, Gretchen is standing in a clearing among the trees, not moving, arms hanging at her sides, chin slumped against her chest, a few strands of hair curling from beneath the hood of her jacket.

"Are you okay?"

"Yes, yes," Gretchen answers. If she is surprised to see him, she does not show it. "But I don't know what to do."

Her voice sounds weak and, for the first time since Wes has known her, unsure.

She sweeps her arm around, gesturing to the ground at her side.

Wes follows her gaze to what first appear to be stones scattered on the snow. Looking more closely, he recognizes a small flock of mourning doves, ten or twelve, feathers so puffed they look like gray softballs. Their eyes are shut, and they could be dead, except for a slight fluttering as they shiver in the cold.

"They should have migrated weeks ago," Gretchen says. "I don't understand how their instincts got so screwed up." She massages the bridge of her nose between her thumb and forefinger. "They'll die out here, and I don't know how to prevent it." She looks up at Wes. "It doesn't seem right, you know what I mean?" and her voice carries the weight of fatigue and grief.

A tough woman to read, he thinks. *She routinely sees animals die. It is the nature of things.*

Wes stuffs his hands into his back pockets and looks up as a thick wedge of moon slices through a break in the clouds. The snow-covered field reflects the temporary glow. Ice-laced trees shimmer both from below and from above, and the lake gives off steam, and Wes experiences fierce awe for this land on which both he and Gretchen stand.

Then he kneels to study the doves huddled together on the ground, and he looks up at Gretchen, her face softened and made beautiful by sorrow. "The truck," he says, removing his jacket and spreading it on the ground, "the heater."

He and Gretchen gather the doves into the nest of his coat. As they stumble back across the field, the snow eases to light flurries that drift in the air like goose down, and the wind calms to a whisper.

He turns to Gretchen as they walk. "You know, you could have frozen out here. What would you have done if I hadn't shown up?"

"I would have done exactly as I did," she says. "I called for help from my cell phone. The wrecker should be here within the hour."

Wes shakes his head at his own stupidity, angry with himself for his needless worry about this self-sufficient woman who neither asked for nor requires his assistance.

"But thank you for being concerned," she adds, and lightly touches his forearm. "That was kind of you."

At his truck, Wes turns up the heater to full blast and sets the doves, still bundled in his jacket, on the front seat. He and Gretchen stand outside waiting for the tow truck and watch the birds for any sign of recovery. Wes crosses his arms at his chest and begins pacing the length of the truck and back to ward off the cold—but he refuses to sit in the truck lest he frighten the doves should they revive. When he pauses by the passenger window, he senses Gretchen move alongside him, and he feels the press of her shoulder against his shoulder as they rest their arms on the truck's roof and bend to look inside.

They stand there in the clearing night, close, neither sure what the next step might be, each alone in the memory of past losses, each considering what of themselves to risk in the future. And from within the truck come the first haunting coos of the mourning doves awakening from their slumber.

Fairweather, Colorado

They all suspected Vera had grown more deaf than she cared to admit and was well along that slow glide into senility, so they waited patiently when she failed to answer straightaway.

Her nieces and nephews, gathered to celebrate her birthday, had just finished a midday meal of baked chicken with mashed potatoes and gravy, fresh shelled English peas, marinated carrots, and hand-squeezed lemonade. George, Vera's eldest nephew on Martha's side, recently retired from his own food-brokerage business, sliced into an enormous white sheet cake decorated with a flag fashioned of one-hundred-three small candles in red, white, and blue.

He passed her a corner piece thickly scrolled with frosting and asked again, "Aunt Vera, what's your secret? Always on the go, never a worry, never a complaint."

The three surviving children of Vera's two dear sisters

▸

sat around the polished table in George's dining room along with a bevy of their offspring. In the living room, an overflow of exuberant youngsters were perched at card tables centered over red plastic cloths to catch scraps flying from their paper plates. It was an airy, cheery setting that Vera had no wish to dampen. Still, the question floated in the air and gnawed at her.

"What keeps you going?" This from someone else at the main table. Vera heard the question without associating a name with the voice.

She remained silent so long, she feared the others must surely think her mind had wandered.

Edna's middle girl—her name escaped Vera at the moment—filled the lapse in conversation. "Never been sick a day in your life, have you?"

And George repeated more loudly in so slow and measured a cadence that the others paused in their meal to glance up at them, "Never a worry—how do you manage?"

Vera's mind had not strayed; she had heard him clearly. She was deciding how to answer. An innocent, chatty question—did it deserve an honest reply or the expected polite blather? In those long moments between his question and her response, Vera stared down at her mummified-like, purple-veined hand curling around her fork and remembered delicate fingers the color and texture of heavy cream. She remembered.

Always on the go, George had said. *Never a worry ...*

August 1918. Vera is moving back in with her parents and two younger sisters until Lester returns from the fighting in France and they can begin their own lives together on the quarter section his father had gifted them upon their wedding. Her infant, Johnny, lies sleeping in the crib beside her bed, his downturned mouth and slightly contracted brow reflecting something of Lester's earnestness. She opens the window of the small room above her parents' mercantile to the unseasonably warm afternoon sun and looks out over Fairweather, named by its founders either in prayerful supplication or in ironic jest. Before her spreads a parched farming town squatting on the dry Colorado flatlands, a town with washboard roads and weather-beaten structures propped against the unforgiving winds with spars of lodgepole pine, a town existing on the fragile edge of subsistence and populated with leathery, hard-edged immigrants.

For a moment, her heart sinks at the sight of her surroundings—the cramped room, the dusty streets, the unpainted clapboard shacks—but then her Johnny-boy stirs, babbles in his sleep, and Vera's spirits rise again at the prospects of her new family. Their land east of town is more than passably fertile, and it contains a small rise from which on clear mornings she can just make out the dim blue haze of mountains on the western horizon. She closes her eyes and feels herself hugged close to Lester, standing on that hillock of bunchgrass with the tawny ocean prairie spreading eastward until it merges with the heavens and the high white peaks barely a possibility to the west. The brisk evening carries the scent of new grass and quenched soil. The world stretches open before them.

"The breeze smells of rain; there'll be a shower," Vera said, looking up from her plate as George began passing cake to the others around the table.

"Well, yes, I suppose it just might shower," said George.

"There's no rain in the forecast," said one of his sisters. "Not a cloud in the sky."

"Just the same … ," said George, his eyes shooting her a caution. "Vera, try your cake, it's delicious. You were about to share your secret for staying young and healthy."

Young … Lester sits at his father's table on Sunday morning, late spring, after planting, reading the weekly newspaper they allow themselves to buy each Saturday afternoon after chores. Vera pours his coffee and stands looking past his shoulder at a caricature of two spire-helmeted Huns standing with their legs spread over a peasant woman huddled in the corner of her small cottage. Their expressions look angry and fierce, their mustaches wild. The peasant clutches an infant to her breast.

"It's not right," Lester fumes. "A man is just a man no matter what his title. It's ungodly he should force his way over those farmers."

"It's not your affair," Vera counters. "They'll get by."

She is frightened by the simpleminded righteousness she hears in his voice. Does he not see it is just a cartoon? She notices a glint in his eyes, not of hatred, but of something more subtle she cannot fully define. Excitement, perhaps, the possibility of adventure, the draw of far places and foreign sights that, but for war, she understands he can never dream of seeing. She tastes bitterness under her tongue, feels an aching behind her rib cage, and she suddenly grows angry with him, and afraid. She knows he will soon be gone, and she will be left in Fairweather. She tries to imagine the French landscape on which his blood will be gambled but visualizes only broad, dull plains and shallow streams, and she wonders where in the world one army might hide from another.

Vera cut into her cake as one of the great-grandnephews flew into the room screaming about someone throwing something and almost breaking the television. She had difficulty following what he was saying because his talk was so excited. One of George's sons pushed back from the table and marched with purpose into the living room. Vera noticed the others turning to her again, expectantly awaiting an answer.

▶ *Fairweather, Colorado*

261

Healthy ... October 1918. A Wednesday, baking day. Vera's mother kneading dough on the flour-dusted counter beside the oven, Vera off to the side, in the washroom, hand cranking laundry from the corrugated steel tub through the rolling-pin ringer, shoulders aching from the repetition, Johnny cooing from his cradle by the kitchen door. Around noon, a commotion in the store out front, the dull thump of shutters pulled closed, the rap of her father's hobnailed boots on the hallway. "Spanish flu reported east of town," he says and takes up his rabbit gun to join the militia in closing Fairweather's borders.

And then silence—no street traffic, no church bells on Sunday, no dust stirring above county roads, no commerce to disturb the quiet. From her upstairs room, Vera can see two sentries at either end of Main Street. They stand with shotguns cradled in their arms, guarding the town against contamination, as if the pellets from their shells could knock germs from the sky like they were pigeons. One customer at a time is allowed into the mercantile—only one at a time—hushed whisperings with her father, solemn tones, rumors of weathered, old homesteaders, tough as Colorado winters, falling to consumption, of entire families racked by influenza. Denver newspapers run dual casualty tallies—one column for flu, another for war.

"The quiet, so still," Vera said.

"Ah, the quiet life. I'm sure it has a lot to do with maintaining health," said George, reaching to pat Vera's hand while nodding his head thoughtfully. "Keep an even keel, peace and calm."

Peace ... Second week in November. The flu plays out, the stores reopen, housebound families gratefully return to work and school, and then, on the eleventh, word of armistice flies across the wires. A spirited crowd builds a bonfire in the middle of Main, and Vera joins in the singing and dancing. Her birthday only two days hence, she pretends the celebration is for her as well, the swirling blur of people, happy, relieved faces. She fails to notice Johnny growing fussy and feverish until he refuses to be put in his crib that evening, so she takes him to bed with her and is awakened later by his heat.

November twelfth. Sponge baths throughout the day, and he responds, though his cheeks remain rosy and splotched. She intends to remain awake that night, to watch over him, but she dozes, the past days so arduous, and she is jolted upright sometime after dawn, not by his heat against her, but by his cold. His cold body. November thirteenth: her birthday.

" ... Always on the go ... "

Wrapped in a shroud of memory, Vera barely registered the words spoken to her until she was startled by a hand on her shoulder. "What? Pardon me, what did you say?" Her fork remained poised to sample the cake.

Across the table, George tilted his head slightly and looked at her with a raised eyebrow.

Edna's child—Beatrice, was it? Or Bernadette? "I said, I don't remember you leading the quiet life. You were always on the go. Ran the store practically by yourself. And still found time to obtain the Eucharist three times a week without fail, didn't you, Aunt Vera?"

"Yes, dear."

On the go ... Searching for comfort, for answers. Why her Johnny was taken. Why Lester returns from the war so filled with his own demons he has no energy to help excise hers. Why he returns as broken-spirited and tormented as she. Why he awakes at night screaming about poison fog and blistered flesh peeling from bone. Why, finally, he wanders off to find his own peace and finds oblivion instead. Why times grow more and more harsh—fourteen-hour days in the mercantile, the dryland farmers buying seed on credit and, brows creased as deeply as their furrowed rows, watching the sky for rain but receiving only the relentless winds that carry off their topsoil in great choking clouds.

Eucharist ... She sits during Holy Communion and wonders at the why of it, praying fervently for deliverance, until, eventually, gradually, her despair shrinks to a single black smudge that only slightly blurs her vision of life and she can once again look with thanksgiving at the small blessings—the smiling faces of her young nieces and nephews she spoils with peppermint sticks from the store, the sense of relief that washes the town when rain comes early in the spring and holds off during reaping …

But always, always, deep in that corner of her soul she dares not explore, the doubt lingers, the nights when she falls asleep dreaming the dreams of the true believer only to awake in terror with a vision of her infant boy, a pallid lump of flesh, his cold, chalky cheeks and his dead eyes staring into a void that turns her faith to ice. Black crow eyes …

In the end, Vera did not answer George truthfully. For the truest truth, the answer to George's question, she now admitted to herself, was that she "kept going," in his words, because she was afraid, she was terrified of dying. The memory of what she saw or, more accurately, failed to see behind those eyes haunted her. Time and again, during sleepless nights, she would cry aloud, "My soul waits for the Lord more than watchmen for the morning, more than watchmen for the morning!" and would listen for a reply but hear only the beating of her own heart, the rattle of breath in her throat.

Although an old woman and lonely much of the time, she harbored no bitterness. She loved her family, the warm, encompassing idea of family, and did not wish to cast dark shadows on this gathering of generations. She recalled the threshing sheds of her youth, the large barns that housed the communally owned machines that wrested grain from husks, that threw the refuse of harvest onto the dirt floor and fed the golden manna into great storage bins. And in the final winnowing of her own life's fortunes, she judged the wheat more plentiful than the chaff. She wished to leave her family a gift on her birthday, something that could somehow balance Johnny's black gift to her so many years before. So she looked up at the assembly watching her expectantly and said in a strong, clear voice, "God's grace. That is what keeps me going. The grace of God."

The small congregation smiled, nodded their heads in affirmation, and continued chatting.

"Grace," she repeated in a voice softer than a murmur, and she wondered at the why of that too, why it seemed bestowed so freely on some and withheld from others. And she had no answer.

Then Vera shook her head slightly, as if recovering from a trance, turned to Edna's girl—Bernice, it was, she was certain now—and asked, "Might there be a sip more lemonade?"

Acknowledgments

If it is true that writing is a solitary pursuit, it is equally true that bringing a book to publication is a collaborative one. To the scores of readers who have provided important comments on early drafts, but especially to those who have been there from the very beginning: Cecile, Dennis, Mechelle; to Jackson Webb and his workshops for early encouragement; to Andrea Dupree and Michael Henry, the visionary founders of Lighthouse Writers Workshop, truly a cultural beacon guiding Denver regional writers; to Sam Scinta and Fulcrum Publishing for their commitment to fiction and for their courage to take on a book of short stories by a little-known writer; and to Katie Raymond, managing editor, the epitome of compassionate professionalism, who treated my stories with great respect and made each one better for her input, my profound thanks.

About the Author

Gary Schanbacher's stories have appeared in numerous journals, including *Colorado Review*, *South Dakota Review*, *The William and Mary Review*, and others. He holds a PhD from the University of Colorado, and he and his wife reside in Littleton, Colorado. *Migration Patterns* is his first collection of short fiction.